*WE WERE THERE*

WITH # THE PONY
EXPRESS

By WILLIAM O. STEELE

Historical Consultant: SYLVESTER VIGILANTE

*Illustrated by* FRANK VAUGHN

GROSSET & DUNLAP *Publishers* NEW YORK

*To the Staff
of the Chattanooga Public Library
with gratitude for able assistance
and long patience*

PRINTED IN THE UNITED STATES OF AMERICA
LIBRARY OF CONGRESS CATALOG CARD NO. 56–5889
*We Were There with the Pony Express*

# Contents

# CONTENTS

[ *vi* ]

# Illustrations

[ *vii* ]

# ILLUSTRATIONS

### ACKNOWLEDGEMENTS

*"I'll eat when I'm hungry"*
*"The hardest work I ever did"*
*"Wish I had a nickel"*
Reprinted by permission of Ruby Terrill Lomax, from John and Alan Lomax, AMERICAN BALLADS AND FOLK SONGS, The Macmillan Company, New York, N. Y., 1934

*"Did you ever hear tell of sweet Betsy from Pike?"*
Reprinted by permission of Ruby Terrill Lomax, from Alan Lomax, FOLK SONG, U. S. A., Little, Brown and Company, Boston, Mass., 1948

*WE WERE THERE*

WITH **THE PONY EXPRESS**

# CHAPTER ONE

## *Off to the West*

---

Hooray for the Pony Express!" yelled a man in a wide-brimmed hat. He drew out his revolver and fired over the heads of the crowd. *Bang! Bang! Bang!* "Whoopy-whoopy-bow-wow! Let this here shindig get going!" he roared.

Another pistol went off. Mark Claggett wished he had a revolver to shoot. Anyway, he wouldn't have dared with his aunt right beside him.

"Let's get out of this crowd before we get shot," Aunt Matilly exclaimed.

"Now, Matilly, we're safe enough," Uncle Hubbard told her. "A little celebration never hurt anybody."

Mark turned and grinned at his sister. "Rose and I like it, Aunt Matilly," he said. "This is the biggest crowd we've ever seen."

[ *3* ]

"Much bigger than the Independence Day celebration we have back home in Harrisville," Rose added.

"Well, this is a great day for St. Joseph," Uncle Hubbard told them, "and it ought to be celebrated. Yes, sir, you can count on it, April 3rd, 1860, is a day folks will long remember. Today the Pony Express is making this country a real United States. It's bringing the states close together. Why, it used to take thirty days or more to get mail from Missouri to California. Now the Pony Express will take a letter from here to the coast in ten days."

"Not if they depend on young rapscallions like that one," Aunt Matilly said, nodding at the young man who stood in the center of an admiring throng. "He can't be more than seventeen and as full of wickedness as a blackberry is of juice."

"Now, Matilly," protested Uncle Hubbard. "Billy Richardson is twenty-three and a fine young man. Every Pony Express rider is a gentleman and he has to swear that he will not fight, drink, or use profane language."

Mark stared at the rider with envy. The young man was dressed in a red shirt, and his blue pants were tucked into the top of fancy boots. He had a white sombrero on his head and a pistol at his hip.

[4]

A real express rider! Mark sighed. He'd never be one. Fourteen was too young. Besides, he'd never ridden anything but his father's old plow horse. That bay pony looked spirited.

A man behind the Express rider suddenly reached out and cut some hairs from the mare's tail. "Get your Pony Express souvenir right here," he cried, holding up the horse hairs. "A real souvenir from the tail of the first pony to carry the mails west!"

Rose sniffed, "Humph! Some men don't care how they make money," she remarked. "I wish the pony had kicked him right hard."

Uncle Hubbard laughed. "That mare will grow another tail, but I don't think much of a man who would do a thing like that."

They watched the souvenir seller move off down the street.

The band on the stand beside the railroad station began to play "March to the Battlefield." A few moments later a man told the crowd that the mail would be late getting to St. Joseph. The Hannibal and St. Joseph train had to wait on the mail train from Detroit.

"While we wait," the man went on, "we will be favored with a few words from Major William Russell, one of the partners in the Pony Express Company, Russell, Majors, and Waddell."

"We'd better go on to the stagecoach station," Aunt Matilly said. "I'm sure these speeches will be very fine, but I'm afraid you children will miss the coach."

[6]

"I wish I could see the special train come in from Hannibal with the Express mail," Mark said. "They say the mail car's going to be painted and decorated specially for the celebration."

"It may not get here at all," Uncle Hubbard told him. "There's just an engine and a mail car coming over those new tracks at a high rate of speed. Personally, I wouldn't be on it for anything. But I hear all the railroad officials are riding in the mail car to show their faith in fast trains."

"I'd rather put my faith in horseflesh," Mark grunted. "Why, I bet the Pony Express won't ever be late!"

They left the crowd at the railroad station. Mark glanced back as they started down the street. He hated to leave the brightly dressed rider and his little bay mare.

"That's a mighty fancy bridle and saddle on the pony," he told his uncle.

"Those decorations are real silver," Uncle Hubbard said. "But it's just for the celebration. Billy will put special light equipment on his bay before he really begins his ride with the mail. Every ounce counts when you're traveling two thousand miles in ten days."

Mark was sorry he and Rose were leaving on the

stagecoach and wouldn't be able to stay for the celebration. There'd be dancing and a fiddling contest tonight. And he'd have liked to see the first Pony Express rider set out.

They walked down streets decorated with flags and bunting until they reached the stagecoach office. The coach stood ready and waiting. The driver and the conductor were already on the driver's seat on top of the vehicle.

"You children get in," Uncle Hubbard told them. "I'll get your tickets and put your valises in the boot."

Rose turned to watch. The "boot" was a leather-covered compartment projecting from the rear of the coach for luggage.

Aunt Matilly bundled them into the coach. "I declare I hate to let you children travel alone to Nevada," she complained. "It's no trip for a twelve-year-old girl like you, Rose. I've half a mind to keep you with me."

"We'll be all right," Mark spoke up quickly. Aunt Matilly grumbled too much, and he'd hate to have to stay here any longer with her. "I'm fourteen and I can look after us, Aunt Matilly."

"Don't worry, Aunt Matilly, we'll be all right," Rose assured her.

Aunt Matilly began to give them all sorts of instructions about what to do and what not to do. Uncle Hubbard stood beside her, grinning.

"Don't forget to use the parasol I gave you," she said. "No refined young lady has freckles. And don't talk to strangers," Aunt Matilly went on. "And don't ever—"

Suddenly the driver cracked his whip. The stage gave a jerk and the wheels began to roll.

"Good-by, Aunt Matilly! Good-by, Uncle Hubbard!" cried Rose and Mark. The coach rumbled away from the station and down the street. "Good-by!"

Mark glanced around. There were three occupants of the coach besides themselves. One was a prosperous-looking businessman. The second was a young man wearing the fanciest vest and four-in-hand tie Mark had ever seen. And the third was a bent and grizzled old man with a ragged beard and bright blue eyes. His clothes were old, and everything about him looked dusty and worn. He settled himself comfortably on the leather seat.

"This here modern kind of travel sure beats the way I came west back in the Forties," he remarked to the group in general. "I was walking alongside a team of slow-poking oxen then."

[*9*]

*Aunt Matilly began to give them
all sorts of instructions*

The businessman looked around at him. "This route was the Oregon Trail then, wasn't it?"

"Yup," the old man replied. "And a dustier, rougher trail I've never been over. Why, I wore out two pair of shoes and three teams of oxen walking to Oregon. That's the reason I appreciate traveling by stagecoach."

"Humph!" the businessman told him. "Wait till the railroads push west. Now there's real modern transportation for you."

"Be fifty years before the trains span the American continent," remarked the old man.

The businessman shook his head. "Oh, I'm sure it'll be much sooner than that," he answered. "Business will demand that the trains come west. And Congress will give the railroads free land and before you know it, this will be civilized country with railroad tracks everywhere."

"Time sure does bring changes," the old man grunted. "But I kind of hate to see trains pushing across the plains here. This is horse and buffalo country. Iron horses will be out of place."

The young man said, "I expect it will be a long time before tracks are laid to the West."

"What do you mean, sir?" asked the businessman.

[ *11* ]

"I mean the coming war will stop the trains," the young man answered. "The iron won't be spared for railroad tracks. It'll be needed for cannon and ammunition."

"You think the North and South will go to war over slavery?" asked the old man.

"I believe so," the younger answered.

"I agree with you, sir," the businessman nodded. "But there are more causes for war than just the slavery question—for example, the disagreement over States Rights. Whenever a state thinks it is stronger than the Federal Government of all of the states, then I believe war is bound to come."

"Yes," the young man agreed, "it'll take a war to settle all the many differences between the North and the South."

"You ain't running away from being a soldier, are you?" asked the old man.

The younger one laughed. "Oh, no, I'm just seeing the sights before the army gets me." He grinned at his older companion and added, "I hope I find the West worth fighting for."

The old man slapped his leg and laughed. "You will," he said. "The West's a great place, no two ways about it."

He turned his kind, wrinkled face toward Rose,

who was straightening her skirts and retying her bonnet strings.

"Well, well, where are you youngsters headed?" he asked. "Don't often see young folks like you on a stagecoach. Are you out to see the sights too?"

"We're going to Egan Canyon," Mark explained. "Our father is there. He's in charge of a Pony Express station and we're going to join him."

"We've been living in St. Joe, Missouri, for a year with our aunt and uncle," Rose went on. "We come from Harrisville, Illinois. Papa went prospecting for gold out in Nevada with a friend of his. But they didn't find any gold or anything. Mother died a year ago and we came out here. Now Papa has got this station and he's sent for us."

"Egan Canyon," the old man repeated. "I've been through there a few times. It's fine country, but you won't have many neighbors except red ones."

"Indians?" Rose's eyes grew big as she spoke. "I'm scared of Indians."

"Well, now, don't be frightened," the old man said. He looked as if he were sorry he'd said something to alarm Rose.

"Don't worry, sir," Mark said. "She has a parasol. And she can use it to keep Indians off, as well as

[ *13* ]

to keep the sun off." He turned and said to Rose in a high voice, imitating Aunt Matilly, "No refined young lady has Indians."

Rose giggled and poked him with her parasol. She settled it by her side. It was a pretty parasol, but it *was* a kind of nuisance. Rose hadn't wanted to put it in the boot for fear it might get torn or dirty. And here inside the stage there seemed no place to put it.

Rose sighed. She almost wished she hadn't brought it. She certainly didn't suppose she'd ever use it out in Nevada.

She looked out the window. The countryside was pleasant, rolling farmland. But Nevada would be different. Dry salt deserts and rocky canyons and wild animals and Indians.

It was going to be exciting, of course, but in her heart Rose was just a little bit scared. She wondered if Mark was scared too. Maybe not. Boys were mostly brave. But just what did lie ahead of them in the wilds of the West?

# CHAPTER TWO

## *The Deserted Station*

---

Hour after hour the coach rolled westward. When darkness came, the leather curtains were drawn across the windows to keep the chill out. All that night and the following day, and day after day, the stagecoach flew along. It seemed to Rose and Mark that they had been riding forever.

Along the Platte River, past Fort Laramie they sped. At one station Mark was surprised to see six mules led up to be hitched to the stagecoach.

"We'll never get anywhere now," he thought. But he was mistaken. The mules could really run. By afternoon they had passed Independence Rock. The following morning they went through the Continental Divide at South Pass.

Later in the day the conductor yelled to the passengers, "Yonder comes the Pony Express!"

Mark leaned out the window. "I see him," he exclaimed. "Boy, he's coming toward us like a cyclone!" This was the first rider they had seen. The others must have passed them in the night, he thought.

A moment later the rider reached the coach. He waved as he rushed by. Mark gazed after him.

Wouldn't it be great, he thought, to be a Pony Express rider and have folks admire you?

On the fifteenth day the children reached the Mormon town of Salt Lake City. Here they left the

Central Overland stagecoach and made their way to the Pony Express offices.

The stagecoach did not go through Egan Canyon. Mr. Claggett had written that he had arranged for them to ride the supply wagon to Egan Canyon. Food for the stations along the Pony Express route and grain for the horses had to be hauled by wagon.

Rose and Mark found the wagon slower and rougher riding than the stagecoach. Nights, they slept in the Express stations on pallets on the floor by the fire.

The wagon driver was a tall, thin man who chewed tobacco all the time. His white beard was stained yellow around his mouth from the ambeer. He never stopped chewing tobacco, even when he was telling the children stories.

He was called Thin Joe by everyone. "And you call me Thin Joe, too," he told Rose and Mark. "I've never been called anything else since I prospected with a man who had the same name as me. Folks got to calling him Fat Joe and me Thin Joe, to keep us straight."

The wagon rattled on day after day south from Salt Lake City, past Traveler's Rest Station, up a dry wash called Pony Express Canyon, and on to Rush Valley.

"Now here is where a whole heap of grain and hay is grown for the Pony Express," Thin Joe said.

It was a beautiful valley. Rose thought how nice it would be to live here where everything looked clean and neat and green.

The following day they went over a mountain range and down onto the desert. Cedar and piñon pines, low brush and greasewood, dotted the arid stretch.

[*18*]

Alkali dust rose from under the wagon wheels and settled over everything. It burned their throats and made Rose cough.

"Keep a handkerchief over your nose and mouth," Thin Joe instructed the girl. He pointed ahead. "See that fine lake ahead? You keep your eye on it."

Rose looked across the dusty country. In the distance was a pool of blue water. Around the edges were trees. On one side was a green mountain. It looked lovely to Rose. She wished she were there now and away from this horrible dust.

Hours later they still had not reached the lake. In fact, Rose could no longer see it. "What happened to the lake?" she inquired. "It's disappeared."

"That was just a mirage," Joe told her. "Ain't no lakes along this stretch, but I wanted to take your mind off the dust and your coughing. That's the reason I pointed it out to you."

Thin Joe held up his arm and leaned away from the girl, as if to dodge a blow. "Now don't hit me, please, Miss Rose," he joked.

Rose laughed. "I won't this time," she told him, "but don't let it happen again."

All three laughed then. The rest of the after-

[ *19* ]

noon they spent picking out strange shapes from the jagged range of mountains near by. They found a monkey and an elephant and a horse.

"Yonder's a donkey with long ears," Mark said. He indicated a mass of rock with two pointed peaks. "Or maybe it's a rabbit," he added.

" 'Tain't neither one," Thin Joe said. "It's a man lying on his back with his feet sticking up in the air."

"I think it's a stove with two pots on it and a spoon sticking up out of each pot," Rose told them.

"Well, now, it does beat all, the things to be seen in mountain rocks," Thin Joe remarked. He got a fresh chew of tobacco. "But I'm going to show you something sometime tomorrow that you'll like."

"What is it?" asked Rose.

"A surprise," the driver answered and that was all he'd say.

The following day Mark and Rose waited eagerly for the surprise. And when they saw it ahead of the wagon they thought it was a mirage.

"Ain't no mirage this time," Thin Joe assured them. "That there is real honest-to-goodness water."

Soon they reached Fish Springs. The children

were amazed at the thousands of minnows swimming in the clear water. It was the kind of place to have a picnic, and Mark and Rose and the old driver ate their meal beside it.

Now their way led toward the West. The wagon jarred monotonously on. "Stagecoach riding was a luxury compared to this wagon," Rose thought. But she didn't let Mark and Thin Joe know how sore and tired she was.

One day Thin Joe turned to Rose and Mark, who were on the wagon seat beside him, and began a story as he always did. "Let old Thin Joe tell you a tale," he said.

Both the youngsters nodded eagerly.

"Once I was a-traveling up a valley and I accidentally knocked off my rifle sight. Well, I made one out of some metal I found handy. And it wasn't till a week later I realized I'd made my rifle sight out of the purest of silver. I tried and tried to find that valley again, but I never did."

"Gosh," remarked Mark. "Silver gun sights!"

"What a shame!" exclaimed Rose.

The old prospector nodded. "Yes, it was, but I didn't let that stop me from prospecting. And I found a vein of gold 'way back in a narrow canyon. Wasn't no way to get a wagon or coach in there

[ *21* ]

to take the gold out. And you know what I did?"

Rose shook her head. "What?" she asked.

"Why, I just melted my gold and molded it into round balls, bigger than cannonballs," the old man said, chewing his tobacco faster. "And then I just rolled the balls down the canyon. Later a Wells Fargo coach picked them up for me at the bottom of the canyon. Smartest dern trick I ever pulled," he laughed.

Mark laughed with him. "That's the wildest story I ever heard," he said.

"But every word of it is true," Thin Joe told him.

As the days wore on, Rose and Mark were glad of the old man's company. His tales made the slow, jolting ride less wearisome.

One afternoon a man on horseback stopped the wagon He spoke to the children and then talked a few minutes to Thin Joe. After he had ridden off, the driver said, "That there be Major Howard Egan. He's one of the best men to work for that I know of. Been riding over the express route inspecting the trail and the stations. He's one of the superintendents, and he knows this country like the palm of his hand."

"Major Egan," repeated Mark. "Is Egan Canyon named for him?" he asked suddenly.

Thin Joe nodded. "Major, he laid out a trail across the deserts of Nevada years ago. The Pony Express decided to use this trail because it is the shortest route to Carson City in western Nevada. And the trail goes right through Egan Canyon."

He chewed a moment in silence and added, "The major rode the first Express mail out of Rush Valley into Salt Lake City, too."

Mark's mouth fell open in amazement. "You mean— Did that old man—" he stammered. Finally he said, "Why, Major Egan looks forty years old at least. I thought the Pony Express only used young riders."

"That's right," the driver nodded. "Takes a young man to stand the hard riding on the Pony Express. And the major is over forty years old. But he's a tough Irishman and he can ride like the devil himself. But he don't ride the Express any more."

About sunset they reached the Deep Creek Station. "We'll spend the night at this home station," Thin Joe told them.

"Is Egan Canyon a home station?" Mark asked.

"No, it ain't," the driver answered. "A home

station is where one rider takes another rider's place. Egan Canyon is a swing station. That's where riders change to fresh horses. There be swing stations every ten or fifteen miles—all the way from St. Joe to the end of the line in California. And after every four or five swing stations there is a home station."

They stopped in front of a big station house. Behind it were several small houses and sheds. From one of them came the bright red light of a blacksmith's open fireplace. There was a big corral to one side with about ten ponies and several mules in it.

"I wish we were staying at a place like this," Mark thought. "There would be something going on all the time. I bet nothing ever happens at Egan Station."

The following morning they were on their way again. Two days later they moved along a dusty road between scattered clumps of greasewood bushes. Before them was a low mountain range.

"Are we going over that?" asked Rose, gazing toward the rocky summit.

"Through and on top of it," answered Thin Joe. "You'll see."

Soon the high walls of a canyon towered on each

[ *24* ]

side of them. The road wound among the rocks and trees. The cliffs seemed to close in on them as the canyon narrowed. The horses slowed as the road became steeper.

"Now this here is Egan Canyon," Thin Joe told them. "And the station is on a meadow 'most nigh on top of these mountains."

"Goodness!" exclaimed Rose, as the vehicle rounded a huge boulder. "I'm glad the station isn't down here. This would be a good place for Indians to hide and shoot at you from behind these rocks and trees." She glanced around as if she expected to see a redskin aiming a rifle at her.

Now they were at the top of the cliffs and the horses broke into a gallop. Mark looked back to see glimpses of the road as it curved off between the walls of the canyon down to the floor.

"Oh, what a lovely meadow!" cried Rose.

Mark turned his head. Before them lay a smoothly rolling expanse of green, dotted with several kinds of wild flowers. In the bright sunshine it looked pleasant and refreshing after their long ride through the bare, dusty countryside.

"Is that the station?" asked Rose in a shocked voice. "Why, it's just a stone hut with a horse lot."

"It'll do well enough for us and the ponies,"

[ 25 ]

Mark answered with a grin. "I don't know of any fine ladies and gentlemen who might be coming to call on us."

"Nice folks wouldn't live in a shack like that," Rose said.

"Aw, quit being such a lady," Mark said with disgust. "Living in St. Joe spoiled you. You didn't put on such airs when we lived on a farm in Illinois."

The wagon stopped before the stone station house. To one side was the corral with three ponies inside. One animal ran up to the wooden fence and neighed.

Rose and Mark jumped out eagerly. "I wonder where Papa is?" Rose asked. The door to the station was open. She looked inside. "Papa!" she called, but there was no answer. She turned to Thin Joe with a worried expression.

"Don't worry none," the driver said. "Your pa is bound to be around close somewheres. While I unload the supplies, you look around and make yourself at home."

Rose took her parasol and Mark got the two valises. They went inside.

There was a table in the middle of the one room which made up the station. Over it hung a kerosene lantern. There was a big fireplace at the far end of the room. A few embers still glowed there.

Rose stood by the table, wondering how she was going to like living in this small place. She decided she might like it fine when it was cleaner. She might as well get into her old dress and be ready to start scrubbing when Thin Joe left.

She turned away. As she did so, her sleeve knocked a letter from the edge of the table. Mark and Rose were absorbed in taking in their new surroundings and in wondering where their father could be. Neither saw the letter tumble from the table and slide into the folds of the parasol.

"Come on, Rose," said Mark. "Let's look for Papa outside."

"I'll have to change my dress first," his sister told him.

When Mark had gone outside, Rose unpacked her valise. She was a tidy person. She very quickly made up her mind where she would keep her few possessions. She hung up her clothes, laid her Bible on a shelf with her comb and brush.

But what should she do with her good dress, her flounced petticoat, and her parasol? She wouldn't be wearing them here at Egan Canyon.

She took off her dress and petticoat and put on a

*"Something has happened to Papa!" he cried*

fresh gingham. As she buttoned it up, she decided what to do with her good clothes.

She wrapped the parasol carefully in the petti-coat, folded the dress on top, laid them both in the valise, fastened it, and stored it away behind some boxes and barrels.

"There," she exclaimed, dusting her hands. She went outside to join Mark.

"The spring's behind the station," Thin Joe called. "Just follow the path and you'll find it. Your pa may have gone after a bucket of water. Go on and surprise him."

Mark led the way off between the yellow pines. A moment later he stopped suddenly. A man was lying in the path ahead of them. There was a gash on his forehead and dried blood in his hair.

"Rose, look!" he cried. "Something has happened to Papa!"

# CHAPTER THREE

## The Express Rider

---

ROSE ran for Thin Joe. The old driver and Mark carried Mr. Claggett to the station and laid him on the bed.

Thin Joe shook his head as he placed his hand on Mr. Claggett's forehead.

"He's got a fever," the wagoner told Rose. "Probably was sick and feverish this morning when he went to the spring. Slipped and hit his head on a rock. He shouldn't have been here all alone. The hostler who came out here with him only stayed a few days and then ran off."

"Why didn't the Pony Express hire a new hostler?" asked Mark.

"Mr. Ficklin, the superintendent in Salt Lake City, has been trying to get somebody ever since,"

Thin Joe answered. "Everybody wants to be a rider, but nobody wants to stay at these lonely stations."

He narrowed his eyes and looked at Mark. "You're a likely looking young feller," he said. "I expect Mr. Ficklin would hire you as hostler."

"Gosh," Mark exclaimed, looking pleased. "I sure wish he would."

"Well, right now you got to be hostler *and* station master," Thin Joe went on. "I've got to leave. Folks are expecting these supplies. But you young 'uns look smart enough to manage alone. Tell you what I'll do. I'll send Dr. Jones from Ruby Valley over to look at your pa. He can tell you what to do for the fever."

"But suppose he gets worse?" cried Rose.

"I don't think he will," Thin Joe replied. "He's tough. Anyway, the Express goes by every few days. You can send for help. Just promise to keep cheerful and not let being alone bother you."

Rose promised. She had been washing the blood from her father's head. Mr. Claggett stirred and moaned.

"Now, Mark," Thin Joe said. "Your pa's got a rifle and a revolver over there in the corner. I've checked them and they're both in working order.

If any mean-looking critter does come around, shoot. Strangers ain't got no business on Pony Express property."

Mark nodded solemnly and followed Thin Joe outside to the wagon. The old man climbed into the seat. Rose told him good-by from the doorway.

"You two will get along all right," he assured them. "But if you have any trouble, send word by the Express rider. Good-by."

The wagon pulled away.

Mark watched the swaying canvas top for a moment, then turned to the stationhouse. He gave it a careful scrutiny. It was a small, square building with a big rock chimney at one end. The roof was wooden.

The walls were built of stone and were very thick. "Well, they won't tumble down when you get mad and slam the door shut," Mark told his sister.

"They look strong, all right, but why aren't there any windows?" she asked.

There were several narrow slits in the walls. These were only a few inches wide and were filled with dried mud. Suddenly Mark knew why there were no windows.

"This is more like a fort than a house," he told

her. "Windows would make it hard to defend. But if we are attacked, we can knock the mud from those slits. And we can shoot out easily, but it will be hard for anybody to shoot inside at us."

"Oh," remarked Rose faintly. A fort meant fighting. She hoped with all her heart there would be no fighting.

Mark swept his arm over the meadow. "You'll like it here," he said. "There are flowers blooming all over the place. Why, this is the biggest flower garden you've ever had."

Rose turned and immediately forgot all thoughts of battles. In Illinois she used to have a small place of her own to raise flowers. But here, she noticed, there were many kinds of flowers blooming on the meadow. At the far edge near the trees was a patch of bright red flowers. It made her feel better just looking at them. She would have to explore in that direction later and see what they were.

"Let's go inside," Rose said. "Papa may wake up and want something."

"All right," her brother answered.

But Mark stood a moment longer, staring off to the distant mountain tops where the sun glinted on snow. An eagle soared up into view from behind the tall peaks. He watched the bird wheel

[ *33* ]

*He strapped the holster around his waist*

against the snow and then float off out of sight.

Then he followed his sister inside the station. The hut was dim and silent.

"It's so lonely here," Rose thought. "And we're miles from the next stations on either side."

Mark saw the fear work into his sister's face. "She's scared, but she doesn't want me to know it," he thought.

He moved to the corner and strapped the holster with the Colt revolver around his waist. He folded his arms and said, "Bring on the robbers, I'll shoot 'em down, one by one."

Rose laughed. "Put that thing away before you shoot us all, one by one," she told him. "I'd be more afraid of you with one gun than a robber with six guns."

Mark laughed with her.

It was true he had never shot a revolver. When his father got well, he would get him to teach him to shoot.

At that moment there was the sound of hoofs. Mark ran to the door. "It's the Express rider coming from the West," he cried. "And there's no pony saddled for him!"

# CHAPTER FOUR

## Flashing Hoofs

---

MARK ran outside. The rider galloped up to the station, yelling, "Where's my pony? Why isn't it saddled and waiting?" He jumped angrily from his horse before the animal stopped. In his hands was the mail mochila.

He glared at Mark as the boy ran to him. "Where's Claggett?" he asked bruskly.

He didn't wait for an answer but went on with his complaints. "Hasn't Claggett learned yet I've got a time schedule to keep? And doesn't he know I'm only allowed two minutes to change horses at swing stations?"

"My father is sick in bed," Mark explained.

"Well, that's a fine to-do," the rider exclaimed. He threw the mochila over the fence and took a coiled rope from a post. "I guess I'll have to catch my own pony," he went on. "And while I lasso one of these critters, you get the key and open the local mail pouch. I reckon you are in charge if your father is sick. And you'll have to sign on the way-bill the time I got here."

Mark nodded and hurried inside. "Rose, help me find a key," he said.

They searched through the station and finally found the key on a shelf. Mark got his father's watch and pencil and hastened out the door.

The rider had saddled one of the ponies. Mark tried the key in all of the pouches. It didn't fit in three of the locks. He thought he must have the wrong key. But the fourth lock turned. Mark took out the waybill and after the last entry he penciled in eleven-ten as the arrival time.

"Put me down as leaving now," the rider called. "I'm 'most nigh ready to take off." He led the pony through the corral gate.

Mark wrote eleven-twenty and placed the way-bill in the pouch. He locked it quickly.

Then he took a moment to examine the mo-chila. It was a square piece of heavy leather. At each corner was a leather pouch in which the mail was carried. He thought it was a clever idea, for the mochila fitted over each saddle and could be taken off or put on quickly. But the cleverest part was that the rider's weight held it in place.

The rider took the mochila and fitted it over his saddle. The pony started off. The rider ran alongside for a moment and swung up on the pony. He was soon across the meadow and out of sight in the canyon.

Mark went inside and told Rose, "Hurry up with my dinner. I'm in charge here now. The rider said so."

"Hush your foolishness," said Rose. "You'll wake Papa."

Mr. Claggett did wake up. He turned and tossed about in the bed. "The Express rider . . ." he mumbled, sitting up and looking wildly about. "He'll . . . he'll be here . . . got to saddle . . ."

Rose went to him and pushed him gently back onto the pillow. "The rider's already gone, Papa," she said. "Mark took care of everything."

"Letter," mumbled Mr. Claggett. "Got to get . . ." Then he was asleep again.

For a minute Rose wondered what he meant. She left the bedside and went to the fireplace. "Well, Mr. Smarty, come and get your dinner," she said to Mark.

*The rider swung up on the pony*

The next morning Mr. Claggett was still sleeping when Dr. Jones arrived. The doctor looked Mr. Claggett over and told Rose not to worry.

"He's all right. The fever's breaking already," he said. "Give him a dose of this medicine every two hours, keep him warm, and send for me if he gets worse."

Rose was sorry to see the doctor leave. It was so lonesome out in that meadow. When Mark was outside, she could hardly stand the silence.

That afternoon Mr. Claggett awoke. "Why, Rose," he exclaimed. "What's happened? How long have you been here?"

"Oh, Papa," said Rose gently. "You've been sick. We got here yesterday and found you lying by the spring. Take this medicine and go back to sleep. We'll talk when you're stronger."

Three days later Mr. Claggett's fever had gone. But his back had been badly twisted in the fall, and he was unable to get out of bed.

"You'll have to saddle one of the ponies, Mark," his father said, as Mark came in with a load of wood. "The westbound rider comes through this afternoon."

"All right, Papa," Mark answered, dropping the

wood on the hearth. "Which pony should I saddle?"

"The sorrel with the four white feet is the gentlest of the three," Mr. Claggett told him. "But even the sorrel is mean, so you be careful, Mark. Rope him and tie him to the fence and you'll find it easier to slip the bridle and saddle on him."

Mark nodded and started for the side door which led directly into the corral. He stopped beside his sister. "Hurry up with that cake you're going to make, Rose," he grinned. "When I get this pony saddled, I'll be hungry as all git-out."

"Yes, sir, Mr. Claggett, sir, I'll get to work right now," Rose laughed. She picked up a cup and moved over to the flour barrel by the side door. She dipped up a heaping cup of flour.

Mark went outside. He took the coiled rope and shook out the noose confidently. He felt sure he could throw the lasso over the sorrel's head.

He advanced on the reddish-brown animal. The pony tried to dodge around the boy. Mark headed him off. The mustang ran toward the open door. Rose stood there watching with the cup of flour still in her hand. At sight of her, the pony drew up short.

[ *41* ]

*The mustang's sharp hoofs flashed above him*

"Quick, Mark. Lasso him!" hissed Rose.

Mark sprang forward and dropped the rope over the pony's head. The sorrel reared into the air with a screaming whinny. He shook his head and pawed at the ground. Mark held on tight to the rope. The pony lunged at Mark, rising again on his hind legs.

Mark took a quick step backward. His foot rolled on the rope and he lost his balance, falling flat on his back. He looked up to see the mustang's sharp hoofs flashing above him.

# CHAPTER FIVE

## *Indians!*

---

FOR a moment Rose was unable to move. She watched with horror as Mark tried to regain his feet and escape from under the sorrel's hoofs. She knew Mark would be killed if somebody didn't save him. She had to do something, but she couldn't think what to do.

Desperately she raised her hands toward Mark. The cup of flour! Suddenly she knew what to do.

She ran out into the corral and threw the flour up into the mustang's eyes. The pony was blinded and startled by the white powder. He snorted in terror and backed away on his hind legs.

"Quick, Mark, roll away!" screamed Rose.

Mark rolled over on his hands and knees. Quickly he scrambled to his feet, panting and wiping the sweat from his forehead.

"Thanks, Rose," he said. "I thought I was going to be chopped to bits by those hoofs, and I reckon I would have if it hadn't been for you."

"Oh, Mark, I was so frightened," Rose said with a shudder. She turned and stared at the sorrel shaking his head near the fence. "Do you reckon I have blinded him with the flour?" she asked. "Oh, I wouldn't want to hurt him."

Mark gave his sister a long look of disgust. Finally he burst out, "Who in thunderation cares? Had you rather I'd been hurt?"

"Oh, no," gasped Rose, "but I hate to think of hurting the pony."

"Aw, rats," grunted Mark.

He moved warily toward the mustang and snatched the rope that was trailing on the ground. Quickly he looped the lariat around the top rail of the fence. The sorrel tried to buck but was jerked back. He swung around and lashed out with his hind legs.

Mark dodged and grabbed the bridle from a post. Cautiously he tried to throw it over the sorrel's head. The pony shook it free.

Again Mark flung it over the animal's head, keeping his eyes on the pony's rear hoofs. The mustang gave a jerk, but the bridle stayed on. Mark quickly buckled it and stepped a safe distance away.

He turned and grinned at Rose. "Whew!" he said. "That much is done and I haven't been knocked senseless yet by those white feet."

"And I don't suppose you will be, either," Rose told him.

"You mean because I'm so quick?" her brother asked, trying not to look too proud of himself.

"No, because you're already senseless," Rose answered. She turned and walked into the station and slammed the door.

Mark shook his fist at the door. "Sisters!" he muttered.

The white-footed sorrel was quieter now. Mark eased up beside him with the saddle. He placed it gently on the animal's back and waited, half-expecting the pony to act up again. But the mustang merely whinnied shrilly and then was quiet.

Mark breathed a sigh of relief and fastened the cinch. Then he led the pony to the front of the station in readiness for the westbound Express rider.

About half an hour later the Express rider galloped up to the station. Mark was waiting with the key. The rider swung down with the mochila.

*The rider swung down with the mochila*

It was the same man who had come by previously. The rider would have nothing to complain of this time. Now Mark had the pony ready, the key in his hand.

"Hi!" the rider called to Mark. "I see you got me a pony ready this time." He grinned at Mark. "I'm Cyrus Platt and I didn't mean to act so rambunctious the other day when I was headed East."

Mark unlocked the pouch and withdrew the waybill. "That's all right," he said.

"Well, you're learning," Platt remarked. "The girth's too tight, but it's not bad saddling for a greenhorn."

The rider loosened the bellyband. Mark locked the signed time sheet back in the pouch. Platt swung up on the pony.

"How's your pa today?" he asked.

"Better," answered Mark.

"Good. See you again," he said. He dug his heels into the horse's side and was gone in a cloud of dust.

Mark went back into the station. His father was sitting up in bed, having some hot tea. "Whew, I'm thirsty, too," Mark remarked. "But I don't want tea. I want water."

"There's the bucket," Rose pointed out. "I wish

we had a dipper. Papa, don't you have a dipper for the water bucket?"

Mr. Claggett looked puzzled. "Yes, I've got a tin one," he answered. "But I can't remember where I put it. It's queer. I must have been feverish several days before you got here. And I can't remember much about those days." He broke off, frowning.

"Don't worry, Papa," Rose said. "I wouldn't try to remember now."

But Mr. Claggett was leaning forward, staring at Mark. "We're rich!" he said excitedly. "I found a gold mine! You know, this part of Nevada is called, 'The Land Where the Indians Shoot Bullets of Gold.' They are supposed to mine their gold in a cave hidden somewhere in this vicinity. And I found it! I found it just before I began work here for the Pony Express."

"Where is the mine, Papa?" cried Mark.

Mr. Claggett's face fell. "I—I can't remember," he said at last. "I remember climbing up. And I remember a tall, black rock that stood in front of the cave. But I can't remember anything else."

"Don't try," Rose soothed. "You'll remember later."

Mark opened his mouth to speak and then

closed it. Rose was right. Papa was too weak to try to recall the mine's location now. But Mark certainly hoped he could remember it later. Imagine! A real gold mine! "I'll buy myself a horse and a revolver with a solid silver handle," Mark promised himself.

Days went by and Mr. Claggett grew stronger. Mark and Rose grew used to the routine of the station and the arrival of Express riders. Mark got better and better at his work with the horses. He even began to be real friends with the sorrel pony, whom he had named "Four Boots."

Sometimes Mark noticed his father staring intently into space. He was trying to remember where he had found the mine. But he always looked discouraged and shook his head. He *couldn't* remember.

One day, in the middle of May, Mr. Claggett was sitting in the sunshine outside the station door. A man rode up to the station and dismounted. It was Ben Ficklin, the superintendent of the Pony Express.

Mr. Claggett introduced Rose and Mark to him, adding, "Mr. Ficklin is in charge of the central section of the Pony Express, with headquarters in Salt Lake City."

Mr. Ficklin bowed to Rose and shook hands with Mark.

"I'm glad to meet you, sir," the boy told him.

Mr. Ficklin looked Mark over. "I'm glad to meet you, Mark," he replied. "I've been hearing about you running the station while your pa was sick. The Pony Express can use young men like you. So I'm putting you on the payroll at twenty dollars a month. Does that suit you?"

"I—twenty—yes, *sir!*" Mark all but shouted at last.

"Good," Mr. Ficklin replied. "Now, Mark, the mail must go through no matter what. I want you to understand that. Russell, Majors and Waddell have given their promise to get the mail through winter and summer, and every rider and station-master and hostler must live up to the company's promise. Understand?"

"Yes, sir," Mark answered. He wanted to look at his sister to see if she had heard the announcement of his job. But Mr. Ficklin went on.

"The mail pouches will only hold twenty pounds of mail," the superintendent said. "At five dollars for each half-ounce, the total value of each mail run is $3,200. The letters and dispatches are written on thin sheets of paper, and then each group of mail is wrapped in oiled silk for protection. Three pouches carry mail from one end of the run to the other. The fourth is for local mail."

It made Mark shiver to think how valuable the mochila was with its load of mail. He would be handling it and he would have to be careful. It made him feel very important. Working for the Pony Express! Wow! It wasn't as good as being an Express rider, but maybe some day he would be good enough and old enough to be one.

"Now, Mark, I'm going to tell you the pledge we make each Express rider take before he can ride for us," Mr. Ficklin continued. "The company expects the station help to follow it too. Here it is:

> " 'I hereby swear before the great living God that during my engagement and while I am an employee of Russell, Majors and Waddell, I will under no circumstances use profane language; that I will drink no intoxicating liquors; that I will not quarrel or fight with other employees of the firm, and that I will conduct myself honestly, be faithful to my duties, and so direct my acts as to win the confidence of my employers, so help me God.' "

"Mark is a good lad, Mr. Ficklin," Mr. Claggett spoke up. "I believe he'll follow the pledge."

"Fine," Mr. Ficklin answered. "Well, I must be on my way with my inspection tour." He bowed again to Rose. "Good-by, Miss Claggett. Keep these station men well fed."

Rose blushed and nodded.

At that moment a short, fat man galloped up to the station. His hair was hanging down to his shoulders and he had a mustache. Mark didn't think much of his looks and wondered who he was.

Mr. Claggett introduced the stranger as a neighbor who lived about ten miles away. His name was Everett Norris.

Mr. Ficklin shook hands with the newcomer and added, "I was just leaving. Good day, Mr. Norris."

"Just a moment, please, Mr. Ficklin," Mr. Norris interrupted. "I have a complaint to make about the Pony Express. Perhaps it would be best if you heard it, since you're the superintendent."

Mr. Ficklin paused and Norris went on, "Back about the middle of April I brought a letter here to send to San Francisco by Pony Express. I have a business there that my brother is running for me. In that letter there were very important instructions for my brother. He was to let me know by re-

[ 53 ]

turn mail about those instructions. It is a month since I left the letter with Mr. Claggett. Today word came to me from another source that my brother never received the letter."

He paused and looked at the station keeper. "I don't think Mr. Claggett sent off my letter," he added. "I haven't heard of a mail being lost."

Mr. Ficklin turned. "What about it, Claggett?" he asked.

Mr. Claggett rubbed his forehead. "I do remember a letter left here by Mr. Norris," he said in a slow voice. His face wrinkled as he concentrated. "But I don't seem to remember what I did with it."

"Don't remember!" exclaimed Mr. Ficklin. "That's very serious, Claggett. No employee of the Pony Express can be careless with mail." He turned to the other man. "Mr. Norris, I will check our records and see if I can locate your letter."

"That's all very well," Norris growled. "But I lost five hundred dollars because of the loss of that letter. I'll never get that back."

Mr. Ficklin placed his foot in the stirrup and mounted. "I'm distressed to hear that, Norris. If I can't find a trace of that letter, Claggett, I'll have to bring in a new stationmaster here. I'm sorry, but the Pony Express cannot have carelessness."

Mr. Claggett nodded sorrowfully. When the two men had gone, Rose said, "I wouldn't trust that man Norris. He looks like he'd make trouble for folks just for spite."

"No," Mr. Claggett assured her. "He's not making trouble. I remember taking a letter from Mr. Norris about the time I got sick with the fever. But what I did with it, I can't say." He rubbed his forehead, looking worried.

"Don't worry, Papa," Rose said, placing her hand on his shoulder. "Everything will turn out all right."

But she didn't really think that. She and Mark talked to each other about the missing Express letter when they were alone. What would happen if Mr. Claggett lost his job? Mark would lose his, too, they knew. Mr. Claggett was still too weak from the fever to start another job. Mark was too young. And they had no money to return to Illinois.

"I reckon we'll starve," Rose told her brother.

"Poor Papa," Mark said. "He's more worried about the disgrace than he is about another job or about starving, either. He hates to think he's failed the Pony Express, and I would, too."

"Well, let's not show him we're worried," Rose instructed. "Be as cheerful as you can for his sake."

Mark and the Express rider, Platt, were now great friends. The boy tried to imitate the rider. He wore his pants tucked into his boots and spoke out of the side of his mouth like Platt. He had even taken to keeping a bowie knife in his right boot like the Express rider.

Rose laughed at her brother and made fun of him, but Mark only grinned in return. He was looking forward to the day he could be a rider. However, he knew that until the missing Norris letter turned up, he had no chance to be employed as a rider.

Still he hoped for the best. Platt was one of the better riders, and Mark figured he couldn't do wrong to imitate him. He even told Platt about his father's gold mine.

But Platt discouraged him. "I've heard that tale about an Indian gold mine," he said. "But I don't believe there's anything to it. I expect your father just had a fever dream about finding gold. Or maybe he *had* found a cave like that once, and the fever made him remember it. So he thought he'd found it near Egan Canyon."

Mark looked depressed. He'd counted on that mine. If his father lost his job, a gold mine would be a fine thing to have handy.

"Cheer up," remarked Platt. "Gold mining's no fun. Be an Express rider—that's the life."

Mark grinned and waved the rider off.

One night in the latter part of May Mark was wakened by a noise outside the station. He sat up in bed, listening. What was it? The ponies were moving about, bumping against the fence nervously.

He got up and put on his clothes. Slipping into his boots, he eased out the side door into the corral. For a moment he stood there shivering in the chill morning air. It was getting light and he looked about. He saw nothing to upset the animals. But their uneasiness was plain to see.

Crouching low, Mark eased along the fence to the small shed where the ponies were fed. He stopped there, listening hard.

Suddenly behind the wooden wall he heard soft footsteps. He cowered back against the feed trough, his heart thundering in his chest.

*"Indians!"* he yelled as loud as he could

## INDIANS!

The footsteps moved the length of the shed. There was a faint creak of the fence as somebody crept between the poles. Then a dark figure stepped into view, not five feet away from where Mark crouched. It was an Indian dressed only in a breechclout, staring straight at him.

Mark sprang up. "Indians!" he yelled as loud as he could. *"Indians!"*

# CHAPTER SIX

## *The Attack*

---

ROSE heard her brother's screams. It startled her so, she jumped out of bed. She stood there on the cold plank floor, half asleep still. For a moment she thought she had been dreaming.

"Indians!" came the cry from outside. It was Mark again.

"Papa!" yelled Rose. "Oh, Papa, Indians have captured Mark. Papa!"

Mr. Claggett was already up. He grabbed his rifle. Moving to a slit in the stone wall, he knocked the mud out. He stuck his rifle through the loophole and fired.

There was an answering burst of shots. Several bullets hit the side of the station. One plunked into the front door with a hollow sound.

Rose stood there not knowing what to do. Indians! She was terribly frightened. "Oh, why did I ever come to Egan Canyon?" she wailed to herself.

Mr. Claggett moved to the far end of the station and fired from another rifle slit.

Suddenly Rose heard the side door squeak. She looked around with alarm. A dark figure stood in the partly opened door. It wasn't Mark, Rose could see that by the dim light of the fire. It was an Indian coming inside the station!

Rose forgot she was frightened. She sprang forward against the door and shoved with all her might. The Indian fell back, but he kept his foot in the doorway.

Rose picked up the heavy beam which was used to bar the door. She brought it down with all of her strength on the savage's foot.

There was a grunt of pain. The foot was withdrawn. Quickly Rose slammed the bar into place. The Indian beat against the door and then left.

Rose leaned weakly against the wall, panting and swallowing with fear. "That was close," she thought. "If that Indian had got in, he would have killed Papa and me. I reckon I saved our lives, and the Pony Express station too!"

She drew a deep breath, feeling better already.

[ *61* ]

*Rose shoved with all her might*

She'd been scared, but not too scared to fight.

"Rose, get the ammunition from the corner," Mr. Claggett called. "Bring it to the table."

Mr. Claggett waited with his empty rifle. "Here, Rose, load this rifle while I keep up a fire with the pistol. You know how. I've showed you." He ran to another rifleport and fired away.

The room was half-filled with gun smoke. The acrid smell burned Rose's nose and throat. She coughed, but she went on loading the rifle in the half-light.

Mr. Claggett now handed her the pistol. He took the rifle, moving across the room. "The ponies are gone," he exclaimed.

Another shot thumped into the front door. The Indians were not shooting so much. Mr. Claggett too only shot occasionally now. But he continued making the rounds of the loopholes.

"I don't believe they can take the station," Mr. Claggett told Rose at last. "We'll be safe as long as the stone walls stand. But Mark's outside! And I'm worried about the Express rider. He's due here soon, but he'll never get through. The Indians will kill him, and there's nothing we can do to warn him."

"Oh, Papa!" cried Rose, wringing her hands.

"What's happened to Mark? Do you reckon the Indians have him? Will they kill him?"

"I don't know. All we can do is pray and hope," Mr. Claggett told her, then added, "and fight the redskins for all we're worth."

Rose nodded her head wearily. She felt as if she had been loading the weapons for years. But tired as she was, she would keep on fighting.

She sat down in the chair and leaned against the table. The Indian guns were silent outside. Sunlight streamed through the rifle slits on the east side of the hut into her face.

Suddenly Rose heard a sharp crackling noise. It sounded like fire, but only hot ashes were in their fireplace. She glanced around the room. Then she leaped to her feet, her eyes wild with fear.

"Papa, the roof! The Indians have set fire to the roof!" she screamed.

# CHAPTER SEVEN

## *Capture*

---

THE Indian lunged forward as soon as Mark shouted. But the boy dodged and sped toward the station, running as hard as he could. The way was clear across the corral. He could see the side door still standing open.

Then he heard running feet behind him. The savage leaped on his back. Mark stumbled forward under the weight, tearing at the arms that clutched his chest. He fell in the dust and rolled over, jabbing the red man in the face with his elbow. He struggled to his feet and pulled himself loose from his opponent.

The Indian grabbed him by one foot. Mark kicked out frantically and felt his hard boot hit the redskin. Now he was free and racing once more for the station.

*The savage leaped on his back*

One of the ponies galloped in front of Mark, tossing its head and neighing loudly. He heard rifle shots. The attack had begun in full.

"Let it begin," he told himself. "Another moment and I'll be safe inside, shooting back at the Indians."

There were several warriors in the corral, driving out the Express ponies. But they were across the corral and not near enough to stop him.

"I believe I'm going to make it," he panted.

Then a small figure streaked along the side of the station.

"He aims to head me off at the door," Mark thought.

He pumped his legs faster. He *had* to get away, or else he would be captured and tortured and killed.

He was panting and tired. He wished he didn't have his heavy boots on. They slowed him up.

The door was just a few steps away. He reached out his hands to shove it open.

Then the little Indian hit him. Mark was knocked into the fence. The warrior was on top of him with his hands around his throat. Mark could not breathe.

Another Indian grabbed his arms and tied them

[ *68* ]

behind him. The little Indian let him go and Mark drew a deep breath.

"They've got me!" he moaned.

Mark was led off behind the station through the pine trees. The Indians' horses were tethered some distance beyond the spring. He was thrown to the ground and his feet tied with a leather thong.

His captor moved off and Mark was alone. The ground was cold, but he was so tired he didn't care. He lay there, listening to the faint sound of firing.

"The Indians have the station surrounded," he said aloud.

Would his father be able to cover all sides of the station against the attack? Or would the savages sneak up close and burst open the door?

"Poor Rose," he thought. "She'll be terrified."

Then Mark remembered the side door. Would Rose think to bar the door? Mr. Claggett might not realize that it had been left open. The savages would get in!

Mark groaned. Rose would be too frightened to do more than cower in the corner. It was all *his* fault.

"I should never have gone out into the corral alone," he muttered. "I should have wakened Papa first and let him cover me with his rifle."

He turned wretchedly this way and that. But how could he have known that Indians were in the corral? It might have been a mountain lion after the ponies, and he could have scared it off.

But Indians! Mark had never really expected Indians to attack the station. He'd heard the Nevada Indians never gave much trouble beyond stealing horses.

"Well, thanks to me, the Indians have the Express ponies *and* the station," he thought.

Mark raised his head, listening carefully. He heard no shots. That meant the battle was over. The Indians had slipped into the station through the side door.

"Now what will the red devils do?" he wondered.

Suddenly he knew. They would lie in wait for the Express rider probably. And Platt was due through soon.

Mark looked up through the pines. He saw the yellow light of sunrise on the top branches. In an hour Platt would gallop up to the station. Mark could not let him be shot and the mail taken.

There was nothing he could possibly do to help his captured father and sister, but he would keep the mail going.

"I've got to get away before the Indians come back here for me," he said. "But how?"

He pressed his wrists against his bonds. He'd never be able to break them.

"My bowie knife!" he exclaimed. "Why didn't I think of it before?"

The Indians had searched him, but they had not thought to look inside his boot.

He rolled over on his back and raised his legs in the air. The knife fitted tightly in the piece of leather sewed inside the boot to hold it. He shook his legs harder. At last, the knife tumbled to the ground.

Mark wriggled along on the ground until his hands could grasp the handle. He held the knife so that the blade was pressed against the leather thongs.

Then he rolled over so that his weight forced the blade into the leather. The knife twisted in his hands and cut his wrist.

"Darn!" he exclaimed. "I've got to do better than that."

Mark tried once more and again he cut himself. The wounds were slight, but they bled freely. The knife handle was slippery with blood now. But he had to go on. He *had* to warn Platt. He got as tight a grip as he could on the knife and rolled over on it.

This time the blade was pressed firmly against the leather. The bonds were cut and his hands were free. Quickly he slashed the thongs around his ankles. He wiped the knife and returned it to his boot.

"Now to get out of here," he said as he stood up.

He listened for any sign of the returning Indians. He heard nothing. But Mark took every precaution, nevertheless. He moved as quietly as he could.

"I'll stop Platt a safe distance down the trail from the station," Mark planned. "Then I can lead him in a wide circle around the Indians so he can get safely started down Egan Canyon."

Mark thought it was a fine plan. He walked on silently toward the west. Suddenly from ahead of him came a faint sound.

What was it? He stopped to listen. Now he heard it plainly. It was a horse galloping over the rocky trail.

"That's Platt with the Express mail!" he cried.

Mark began to run. He couldn't move very fast, because he was tired and his legs ached from being tied up. In and out between the tree trunks he went. He wasn't sure he was going to be able to keep going.

Platt must be very near, for Mark could hear the horse's hoofbeats clearly. He was suddenly terrified that he was going to be too late to stop his friend. The Indians would shoot the rider!

Mark forced his weary legs to move faster and faster. He swerved to the left, hoping to reach the trail ahead of the Express rider. He heard the horse speed past just before he burst through the bushes and willows onto the trail.

Too late! Platt was past him and headed for the station. Mark tried to yell, but he was gasping for breath.

"Hey! Platt!" he called desperately. But it was only a feeble squeak.

# CHAPTER EIGHT

## Gold Bullets

---

MR. CLAGGETT pulled the table to the corner of the hut where the roof blazed. He stood on the table and chopped at the wooden roof. A piece of the burning plank fell to the floor.

"Quick, Rose, throw it into the fireplace," Mr. Claggett yelled. He kept on chopping at the roof.

Rose darted for the shovel. She scooped up the fiery chunk and dropped it into the ashes on the hearth. Mr. Claggett hacked off another hot brand. Rose got it up before the pine floor caught fire.

"Now, get me the water bucket, Rose," Mr. Claggett ordered.

He took the bucket and doused the contents on the roof around the charred hole. "There," he said, getting down. "The fire's out, but we'll have

*An Indian suddenly appeared in the hole in the roof*

to keep an eye on this hole. It's big enough for an Indian to get through."

Mr. Claggett went back to watching from the rifle slits. A short while later there was a rustling sound from the corner. The painted face of an Indian suddenly appeared in the hole in the roof.

Mr. Claggett was ready. He fired quickly and the Indian disappeared. "Well, I don't reckon they'll try that again," he said grimly. "I'll get every one that shows his head there."

The two of them waited fearfully. Every moment they expected the Indians to renew their attack. The hours of the morning dragged slowly by.

By mid-morning Mr. Claggett wondered if the Indians had gone. "But I'm not going out to see," he added.

Rose built up the fire and cooked her father some breakfast. She was too tired to eat. Her head throbbed and her throat burned from the smoke. And she was frantic about her brother. But she avoided mentioning him to her father.

Mr. Claggett sat staring into space and she knew he was nearly exhausted. He'd lost the Norris letter and would probably lose his Express job. He'd forgotten where the mine was, and now Mark was captured by Indians. It was all just too much.

Rose dropped her head on her arms, resting on the table. She wished she'd never heard of the Pony Express. It had brought all of them nothing but misery.

"Eat your breakfast, Rose," Mr. Claggett urged gently. "You've fought very bravely, but you can't keep fighting on an empty stomach. And we must be prepared for another attack."

"All right, Papa," she answered. "I'll try, but I don't think I can swallow a thing."

At that moment a horse neighed outside the station. Mr. Claggett sprang up with his rifle. He rushed to one of the gun slits.

"Why, it's Mark!" he exclaimed. "And he's leading Four Boots."

"Mark!" Rose screamed.

She threw open the front door. There stood her brother, his face dirty, his clothing torn, and dried blood on his hands. But it was Mark and he was grinning from ear to ear.

Rose threw herself into Mark's arms. "Oh, Mark, you're safe!" she cried.

"Of course I'm safe," he said loftily. "I'm perfectly capable of taking care of myself."

"We thought the Indians had you, Mark," Mr. Claggett gasped. He put his arm around Mark.

[*78*]

*Rose threw herself into Mark's arms*

"I thought the Indians had *you*," Mark confessed. "And they did have me. But I got away." He told what had happened.

"I yelled at Platt after he passed me," he ended. "I thought he hadn't heard me, but he was on the lookout for trouble. He heard me and looked back. Then he stopped and I told him the bad news. I went with him around the station and through the woods to the canyon. I'm sure he made it safe and sound to Schell Creek Station."

"Did he just come?" Mr. Claggett asked anxiously. "Was he late?"

"Oh, no, it was over an hour ago," Mark answered. "I waited to be sure the Indians were gone. Then I came on. And Papa, I found Four Boots wandering in the woods. He's been shot! Can you help him?"

Mr. Claggett bent and inspected the pony's leg. "It's not a bad wound," he remarked. "But he won't do any running for a while. Fetch me the turpentine bottle, Mark, and while I doctor the wound, you eat some breakfast."

Mark did as he was told. While he was eating, Rose stood at the hearth, glancing at him out of the corner of her eye.

"Humph!" she said to herself. "Maybe he got

captured and escaped. But I was brave too. Papa said so."

Mr. Claggett came in and sat down with Mark. "I'll have another cup of tea, Rose. And you'd better have one, too."

He told Mark, "Rose couldn't eat much breakfast, but she could certainly fight Indians. She's a real Pony Express girl."

Mark glanced at his sister. "It's hard to believe," he said with a grin. "I expected to see the station nothing but a heap of stones. I thought Rose would shiver and shake so, she'd knock it down."

Rose's eyes filled with tears. "Oh, Mark, that's not fair!" she cried. "I *was* scared. But not too scared to fight. And I kept an Indian from coming in the door when you went out and left it open."

"I was worried about that door," Mark confessed. "I was afraid the savages would get in before you got it shut and barred."

"Why, Rose," said Mr. Claggett. "I didn't see that. Tell me about it."

So Rose told her story. Mark patted her shoulder and said she was true blue. Rose smiled happily. She *was* a heroine and they *were* proud of her.

"She's the finest girl in the whole West," Mr. Claggett cried proudly. "I never realized that door was open. I reckon the Claggetts kept the Pony Express running on time today!"

"I'll go look at Four Boots," Mark said. He got up and moved toward the doorway. "I've had so much practice running today, I think I'll hire out to the Express Company as a pony and carry the mail myself."

He stopped and looked at the bullet holes in the door. "They really shot the lead at you. This door is riddled in two dozen places. Hey!" he remarked suddenly. "What's this?"

He got out his knife. Mr. Claggett came up behind Mark as he dug a bullet from the thick wooden door. He held the bullet up. It shone yellow and bright.

"Gold bullets! The Indians were using gold bullets!" he exclaimed.

# CHAPTER NINE

## *Four Boots Finds a Master*

---

IT SEEMED very strange at the station with only Four Boots in the corral. Two days later three new ponies were sent over from Ruby Valley. The ones the Indians had taken were never seen again.

Now Mark had his hands full with the new ponies, for they were nervous and wild. Often it took both Mr. Claggett and Mark to saddle one for the Express rider.

A week later, the first day of June, Thin Joe stopped his supply wagon in front of Egan Station. Behind him were two other wagons and an armed guard of ten men.

Mark met him at the door. "Howdy, Thin Joe," he cried.

"Why, young 'un, I figured the Injuns had you

by this time," the wagoner remarked. "But I'm sure glad to see they ain't."

Mr. Claggett followed Mark out the doorway. "Well, I wish we'd had these men up here last week when the Indians attacked us," he said.

Thin Joe smiled. "Now, the way I heard it, you and that pretty little girl and that boy of your'n made them Injuns sorry they ever come by Egan Canyon," he said. "Mr. Ficklin was mighty proud of the way you saved the station and got the mail through."

"Mr. Ficklin!" exclaimed Mr. Claggett. "Does he know?"

"Cyrus Platt's been spreading word around about your fight," Thin Joe said. He reached in his pocket and drew out a crumpled letter. "Here's a letter for you, Mr. Claggett, from Mr. Ficklin."

Thin Joe turned and hollered, "You, Jones, get that flour and bacon and coffee inside. Hoffer, you unload the grain for the horses."

Mr. Claggett took the letter and went inside to read it. Mark watched him worriedly. "Well, I guess Papa is fired," he said in a low tone.

"Oh, I wouldn't worry about that," said the wagon driver. "Mr. Ficklin was sure enough pleased with your pa for saving the station. Besides, after this Injun raid, it'll be some time before the Express Company will be able to persuade folks to take over these lonely stations. Your job's safe at any rate till folks forget about this Injun trouble."

Mark smiled optimistically. "I hope we get to stay on," he said. "I don't know what we'll do if we have to leave."

"Shucks, don't worry none," Thin Joe told him. "Sit down there and let me tell you about this here Paiute war."

He spat tobacco juice and went on. "These Nevada Indians is generally right peaceful critters, but seems some of them were treated wrong. And they took to the warpath. All the way from Salt Lake City to Carson City in western Nevada the Paiutes attacked the Express stations. Some of the station keepers have been killed and scalped, a whole heap of the stations burned, and a lot of horses stolen."

"You reckon it'll last long?" asked Mark.

"Naw," Thin Joe assured him. He turned and called, "Jones, don't forget, a sack of rice and one of dried peas goes inside too."

The old driver turned back to Mark. "Them Injuns have already done their best to stop the

Pony Express and drive the settlers from this here country," he went on. "But there ain't enough Paiutes to do it. They got few guns and little enough courage. Oh, they might make a few more attacks on the riders galloping along. But it's a safe bet the Injun's grass-fed horses can't catch these fast grain-fed Express ponies."

Thin Joe chewed a moment, then continued, "And the Injuns can't shoot straight enough to hit a flying Pony rider. So I ain't going to give the Paiute war no more thought myself." He added, "Just the same, we're leaving you plenty of ammunition and another rifle. Get your pa to teach you to shoot it."

"I sure will," Mark exclaimed. "Thin Joe, look at this."

Mark took a leather pouch from his pocket and poured out a handful of gold bullets. He'd pondered over the gold bullets a lot. To him, they proved that his father had really found the mine. Cyrus Platt had been wrong. The Indians did mine gold somewhere close by.

"The Indians were using gold bullets to shoot at us," Mark informed the wagoner.

"Well, what do you know about that!" the old man exclaimed. "They didn't have any lead for those old-fashioned muzzle loaders, so they used the only metal they had—gold. I've heard tell they did that sometimes."

Mark started to add that his father knew where the Indians' gold mine was. He caught himself just in time.

It would sound awfully silly to say that Mr. Claggett couldn't remember where the mine was. It would sound like a lie. Besides, there wasn't any point in spreading the news around—not till he'd found the mine again and staked a claim.

The unloading was finished at last, and Thin Joe climbed back in his wagon. "Don't I make a good boss?" he called to the Claggetts. "Never helped a lick with the unloading."

[ *87* ]

He winked at Mark and drove off. The armed guard moved off alongside the wagons.

Mark turned to his father. "What was in the letter, Papa?"

"Mr. Ficklin has placed me on probation for losing the letter," Mr. Claggett replied. "I can stay on and work, but the next mistake I make, out I go."

Rose turned to her brother with tears in her eyes. "It means Papa is in disgrace, and they think he's no better than a thief," she said.

"Thin Joe said to tell you not to worry," Mark told his father. "He said everything would come out all right."

"He's a good old man," Mr. Claggett answered. "But I am worried. I hate to think Norris lost money on account of me. If I could remember the location of that mine, at least I could pay him back."

He frowned and shook his head. "And I hate to have the Express Company think I let them down," he went on. "Where in the world do you reckon I put that letter when Norris gave it to me?"

"I think I'll clean up the station today, Papa," Rose said. "And I'll look everywhere."

"I'll go out and curry Four Boots," Mark remarked. "I wonder what the Express Company will do with him? The wound's healing, but I don't think he'll ever be really fast again."

Mr. Claggett didn't answer. He stood gazing out across the meadow with the same worried expression that the children had noticed so much lately. They left him without a word.

Rose fetched water and gave the hut a good scrubbing. She moved everything, searching for the letter.

"I've looked everywhere," she told Mark with a sigh, "and it's not here."

She pushed her valise with her foot. "No use looking in *there*. I packed my clothes away carefully." She added, "Besides, we got here after the letter was lost."

In spite of all her efforts, Rose did not find the missing letter. Mark soon forgot about it. He had a letter of his own about which to worry. When Four Boots' wound healed up entirely, Mark wrote Mr. Ficklin. He wanted to know what to do with the pony.

The next time the Express rider came by, Mark had the letter ready. He placed it in one of the pouches of the mochila.

"Now make sure you get the mail through to-day, Cyrus," Mark told the rider. "This letter is about Four Boots, and it has to get through."

"I don't know why you bother about that pony," Cyrus replied. "He ain't fit for nothing but coyote meat now."

"You mean that?" asked Mark.

Platt grinned. "Not exactly," he answered. "But I don't ever want you to saddle him for me. He hasn't enough speed for Express duty since he was wounded."

He swung up on the fresh mount. "I don't expect Mr. Ficklin cares what happens to him," he said. "And he might write back and tell you to shoot the pony and eat him."

"I couldn't eat Four Boots," Mark replied. "Even though he won't let me ride him yet, I feel like we're friends."

"I ate horse meat once," Platt said. "Had to."

"Was it like any other animal meat?" asked Mark curiously.

"Just about, only horse meat tastes sweeter," Platt answered. He dug his heels into the pony's sides. "See you another day, Mark," he called back.

Mark turned to the station. Rose was standing

[ *90* ]

in the doorway. "What did he say about horse meat?" she asked.

"Cyrus said for you to figure out the best way to cook horse meat," Mark replied. "He said we'd have to shoot Four Boots. And you've been wanting some fresh meat lately."

A look of horror spread across Rose's face. "Ugh, I couldn't, Mark," she said. "Don't talk about eating horseflesh."

Mark chuckled. "Still the lady, eh?" he asked. "Miss Rose turns up her nose at good horse roast." He moved past her. "Well, we'll soon see what Mr. Ficklin wants me to do with Four Boots."

But when Rose turned away, Mark looked sober. It wasn't that the idea of eating horse meat was so disgusting to him. But he had grown to love Four Boots with all his heart. Suppose Mr. Ficklin ordered him to shoot the pony, or sell him. What could Mark do?

The boy waited expectantly for the superintendent's reply throughout the rest of June. His father told him the pony probably would be taken and broken to harness and used to pull the supply wagon.

"Surely they wouldn't treat a pony which had

carried Express mail that way," Mark retorted. "Mules would be better anyway."

"Maybe so," Mr. Claggett agreed. "But I doubt if Mr. Ficklin will let him stay on here. There's not much point in the station feeding a pony that isn't fit to do the work."

Mark nodded. "Maybe I can buy him," he said to himself. He went and counted his money. The boots had taken most of it. There was little left. "There's not enough to buy Four Boots," he thought.

Then one July morning Platt swung down off a pony. "A letter in the pouch for you, Mark," he said casually.

Mark grabbed the mochila and tried to insert the key in the lock. His hand was trembling. What would Mr. Ficklin say? Would Four Boots be shot? At last he opened the local mail pouch and took out his letter.

"No time to read it now," Platt teased. "Come on. Sign the sheet and let me get going."

Mark tore open the letter. His face fell. "Mr. Ficklin says they usually dispose of the unfit animals in Salt Lake City," he told Platt. Then he stopped. His eyes flew back and forth over the lines as he read further.

*He was admiring his pony*

Suddenly he whooped. "Yipppeeeee! The pony's mine!"

Mr. Claggett and Rose rushed outside. "What's happened?" they inquired.

"Mr. Ficklin wrote me that I could have Four Boots for my very own," he shouted to them. "And free for nothing for being such a good hostler."

"Mr. Claggett," called Cyrus, "would *you* mind signing the time sheet so I can get on? Mark is so happy, he can't be bothered with me."

Mr. Claggett grinned back at the rider. Platt rode away, but Mark didn't even notice. He was standing at the corral fence admiring *his* pony.

# CHAPTER TEN

## *A Race with the Express Rider*

---

THAT summer was one of the happiest that Mark remembered. He did his work at the station. The rest of the time he spent with Four Boots.

Shortly after the mustang became his, Mark decided the time had come to try to ride him. "What's the use of having a pony if you can't ride him?" he asked his sister.

"A broken arm won't be fun, so you be careful," Rose cautioned him.

"Yes, ma'am, Miss Rose," Mark answered in a mock-humble tone. "I'll be careful. I know I'm made of Dresden china with ruffles on it, and I break awful easy." Then he added with a chuckle, "Why don't you whisper in Four Boots' ear that you don't want your brother hurt? Then maybe he'll let me ride him."

[ *95* ]

"Not me," she replied. "I'm the cook and I'm not getting near that wild thing."

"Shhhh!" cautioned Mark. "If Four Boots hears you call him a 'wild thing,' he won't like it. He'll be mad."

"Well, don't just stand there. Go on and get it over with," Rose said. "I want to know whether I'll have to fix supper or fix your broken head."

Mark went into the corral. Rose came outside and sat on the top of the fence.

Mark got the bridle on the pony without any trouble. But the minute he came toward the sorrel with the saddle, Four Boots began to snort and back away.

Mark kept talking to the animal. "Now, Four Boots, that's no way for *my* pony to act," he said in a low, soothing voice. "Come on now, boy. Steady. Let me put the saddle on you."

Mark finally quieted the mustang. Then he picked up the saddle again and tried to ease it on the pony's back. The minute it touched Four Boots' back, he bucked it off.

At last Mark got the saddle on. He left it on Four Boots so the mustang would get used to the feel of a saddle again. He walked to the fence.

"I don't think Four Boots understands English," Mark complained. "He won't do a thing I say."

"He's just too mean to be a saddle horse," Rose remarked. "You'd better trade him off."

"I wouldn't trade him if he stamped me half to death," Mark told her. "I like Four Boots, and sooner or later I mean for him to like me."

Mark moved off toward the sorrel. "Remember I don't have any flour with me today," Rose called after him. "If you get in trouble, you'll have to get out by yourself."

Mark didn't answer. He sidled up quietly to the animal. After a long while of stroking the sorrel, he climbed carefully into the saddle.

He had just slipped both feet into the stirrups when Four Boots bucked and twisted. Mark grabbed the saddle horn and held on tightly.

Four Boots began to buck in a circle. At the third jump Mark went flying through the air. He hit the ground with a jolting thud.

He was on his feet and scooting out of the corral at once. At the fence he looked back. Four Boots was standing calmly in the middle of the enclosure.

Mr. Claggett called from the door, "I have heard that if you starve a horse for a few days you can break him that way."

"I'll try it," Mark said.

That night Four Boots was given neither hay nor corn, nor the following morning either. When Platt rode in with the mail at noon, Mark told him how he was handling the mustang.

"That's no good," Cyrus said. "Starving a horse only breaks his spirit. And a horse with no fight and no spirit is worthless."

"Well, what can I do then?" Mark wanted to know.

"I've heard of Express riders who go up to these wild Express mustangs and hit them across the nostrils with a whip once," Platt said. "That lets the ponies know who the boss is."

"I just couldn't do that," Mark told him.

"Well, you just have to keep on trying," Cyrus advised him, as he fitted the mochila on. "Let Four Boots know you aim to ride him no matter what he does. I think kindness always helps, myself. But don't give in to him or let up in your efforts, Mark. A horse that finds out he can get away with things will keep on doing them till finally he'll become an outlaw horse. And if that happens you'll have to get rid of Four Boots."

Platt rode off. Mark stood staring after him. Everybody had advice to give him. Now he didn't know what to do. He walked to the fence and gazed sorrowfully at the sorrel.

He didn't believe he ought to whip the mustang. He'd heard that you whip a mean horse. Four Boots wasn't ornery. There was no meanness in his ways.

The boy climbed through the fence and took the saddle off. Then he took an old sack and began to rub the pony down with it. He knew Four Boots liked this by the way his nostrils twitched with every motion of the rubbing.

Then Mark fed the sorrel. "Now," he told the pony. "I've been good to you, you start being good to me."

From that day on Mark spent long hours rubbing the pony's nose and stroking his ears and forehead. He kept the saddle on Four Boots while he did this. Some days he left the saddle on the pony while he walked him around the corral.

Each night he was well fed and rubbed down with an old sack. The pony no longer objected to the saddle.

Then toward the last of July Mark thought the time had come to try to ride Four Boots again. The sorrel seemed much tamer now.

Mark approached Four Boots as usual, talking soothingly to the sorrel. He stroked his ears and nostrils and rubbed his cheek gently. Then he eased himself up into the saddle. He sat holding on tensely and waiting for Four Boots to buck.

But nothing happened. Mark patted the pony's neck and rode around the corral. Day after day he rode the mustang, but he did not tell Platt of his success.

One afternoon Mark waited at the far side of the meadow on Four Boots. As soon as the Express rider left the canyon, Mark yelled to him.

"I'll race you to the station," he called.

Platt waved agreement and loped away. Mark leaned forward and patted his pony's neck. "Come on, Four Boots," he urged. "Let's beat Cyrus and that no-good Express pony."

Four Boots galloped off. Faster and faster the sorrel went, side by side with the Express pony.

But then Platt began to gain. He pulled away from Mark, a half a length, now a full length ahead.

"Come on, Four Boots," Mark yelled. The sorrel seemed to fly across the meadow. He began to gain. Now he was almost neck-and-neck with the other pony.

Platt was whipping his mustang, trying to get more speed out of the animal. But they dashed up to the station together.

Platt praised Mark highly. "You've brought that sorrel along nicely," he told the boy. "And furthermore you've got yourself a mighty good pony."

Mark was pleased at his friend's words. As soon as the rider left, Mark went over to Four Boots and put his arms around the pony's neck. "You're the best," he whispered happily.

# CHAPTER ELEVEN

## *Sneeze on Tuesday*

---

AUGUST slipped by and there was no trouble. The mail went through on time and often ahead of schedule. September came with sunny, pleasant weather.

One day, Rose and Mark sat outside the hut in the sunshine. Mr. Claggett was taking a nap. It was a warm day, and white clouds were piling up over the mountains to the south.

"Rose, how about getting your ladylike parasol and holding it over my face?" Mark said sleepily. "This sun's too bright for me to go to sleep." He yawned.

Rose was sewing. She held up her thread and carefully poked it through the eye of her needle. She knotted the thread.

"I believe you've got some kind of yawning fever, Mark. You yawn all the time," she said.

"Well, don't do to me what one of our neighbors in Illinois did when his horse took to yawning a lot," Mark laughed. "He said he knew how to cure his horse. So he put a board on the horse's head and banged on the board with a hammer."

"I don't remember hearing about that," Rose said. "It sounds like an awful way to treat a horse. Did it cure the yawns?"

"No, it cured the farmer," grinned Mark. "The horse ran away and was never found. The farmer said he wouldn't try that cure again."

"Served him right," Rose snapped. "Anybody who'd treat a horse so cruelly! Darn it! I broke my thread."

Mark watched her as she threaded the needle again. He was certainly glad he didn't have to sew that patch on his breeches. He'd wear them with a hole in them first.

Rose took a few stitches. Suddenly she sneezed. She turned to Mark and asked, "What day is this?"

"Tuesday, why?" questioned her brother.

"Didn't you ever hear this rhyme?" she asked.
*"Sneeze on Monday, sneeze for danger,*
*Sneeze on Tuesday, meet a stranger."*

Mark closed his eyes with a grunt. "That's just girls' foolishness," he muttered. "Not many folks ever travel this way. Strangers are as scarce as hen's teeth."

Rose sighed. It was true they seldom saw strangers. But Mark was so sure of himself. Suddenly she laid down her needle.

"If a stranger comes through here some time today, will you sew this patch on your old pants?" she asked.

"Sure," Mark answered with a grin. There wasn't a chance he'd have to do it. Nobody ever came to the station except the Express people, and it was not time for either the rider or the supply wagons.

"All right, then, we'll see," said Rose. She went inside the station, and Mark promptly forgot about the whole thing.

That evening a chilly wind sprang up. The clouds Rose had seen mounting in the sky turned black and threatening. Rose shooed her few chickens under the pony shed. Mark had brought them to her as a present from Ruby Valley the week before. Now she turned to watch Mark pour corn into the feed boxes.

The wind scudded across the meadow as they

went back inside the station house. The fire was warm and cheerful. Rose shut the door and raised the bar. She was glad to shut out the stormy night.

By bedtime the wind was really howling. All three Claggetts had been peacefully asleep for more than two hours, when Rose awoke. Above the sound of the wind she heard a horse stamping outside the door. Who could it be? No Express rider was due.

Suddenly, heavy knocking sounded through the station!

Rose drew the covers up. She heard Mark spring out of bed. She heard her father fumble for his rifle.

"Who is it?" called Mr. Claggett.

"It's Jim Johnston, Mr. Claggett. I've come from Ruby Valley," a deep voice answered. "Me and my pal are about to get caught in the storm. My horse has strained a leg and we want a night's lodging."

"Why, certainly," Mr. Claggett answered.

He opened the door. Two dark figures stood in the doorway. Mr. Claggett stepped out into the windy night.

Rose knew he was helping the two men unsaddle the horses and release them into the corral.

*Two dark figures stood in the doorway*

Papa was always helpful and friendly to strangers.

But she couldn't keep from worrying a little. She'd never heard of Jim Johnston. Suppose the men were really bandits who had lured Papa outside to kill him!

She sat up in bed to call to Mark. He could get one of the rifles and protect them.

She was relieved when all three men came back into the hut. Mr. Claggett got out blankets and the two newcomers lay down in front of the fire.

Mr. Claggett went back to bed. Soon he was asleep. Mark was asleep too, Rose could tell. But what about the two strangers by the fire? Were they sleeping?

Or were they waiting for all the Claggetts to go back to sleep before they got up to kill the station-master and his children and rob the station?

Rose strained her eyes and ears. Did she hear them snoring? The wind and rain lashed the little hut. Finally, in the dim firelight, Rose saw one of the men throw back his blankets and softly rise to his feet!

# CHAPTER TWELVE

## *The Two Strangers*

---

ROSE tried to scream, but she couldn't. Her throat was too dry and she was so frightened, she could barely move.

"I've got to warn Papa and Mark," she thought.

But it was useless. All she could do was lie there and watch the strangers murder her father and brother.

The figure moved toward the beds in his stocking feet. He didn't make a sound. He stopped and looked right at Rose.

Rose shrank against her pillow. Could he tell she had her eyes open and was watching him?

The stranger moved to the table. He ran his hands across it. Rose could hear the forks and spoons rattle.

[ *109* ]

"He's after a butcher knife," Rose thought. Her throat tightened so that she could hardly breathe. "He's going to stab us, one by one. Ohh!" she moaned to herself.

The man suddenly bent down. Rose heard a scraping noise. He was picking up something and shoving it into his mouth.

Why, it was the cornbread left over from the Claggetts' supper! The stranger hadn't been looking for something to use as a weapon. He'd been looking for something to eat.

Rose lay back with relief. Her heart quit pounding, and she could swallow easily now. She smiled to herself in the darkness. What a fright she'd had! And how glad she was she hadn't screamed. Mark would have teased her forever after. She almost giggled. She forgot the newcomers and fell asleep.

The following day was rainy and windy. After the ponies were cared for and wood for the fire brought in, there was no more work to be done around the station. The two men did not want to ride on in the bad weather. Besides, Jim Johnston's horse was still limping.

"I'd like to give him a day's rest, if it ain't imposing on you," Jim told Mr. Claggett.

"We're glad of your company," Mr. Claggett answered.

The five of them sat around the hearth, listening to the wind outside and talking. In daylight the strangers looked young and harmless. The fat one was Jim Johnston. His eyes, Rose noticed, kept going to the table. Rose had left some biscuits there on a tin plate covered with a cloth.

She turned her head to keep from laughing. Jim Johnston was still hungry. Yet he had put away more breakfast than any two of the others.

"Mr. Johnston," she said, "help yourself to another biscuit. If you're hungry, I'd like for you to have them. Mark throws my left-over biscuits at the buzzards and says even those awful birds won't touch them."

Jim Johnston laughed. "Miss Rose," he said, "you have discovered my weakness—eating." He patted his bulging waistline. "It's the reason I had to quit riding them little Express mustangs. I was breaking the critters' backs."

He threw back his head and laughed heartily. His friend, Wilson Thomas, grinned. "It's the truth, folks," he assured the Claggetts. "Jim was light enough to ride for the Express when they started in California. But he took an eating spell. And soon the Express ponies got together and signed a petition asking the company to fire Jim."

Mark and Rose laughed aloud. The idea of ponies writing a petition and lining up to sign it was funny. But then everything about these two was laughable.

Mark thought a lot of Cyrus Platt. But still he wished he'd been at a station where this happy-go-lucky rider, Jim Johnston, had ridden.

It was true about Jim's eating too. At every meal he ate and ate. "I reckon you must be the champion eater of the West," Mark said.

"Well, I just guess he is," Wilson spoke up.

"Jim, tell the folks about the flapjack-eating contest you won."

Jim tilted back on the block of wood on which he sat. "Me and a fellow named Lomax set out one Sunday in Sacramento to see who could eat the most flapjacks," he said. "When the stacks of cakes were set in front of us, I slipped a dead grasshopper between the hot cakes about four from the bottom of his second stack."

He stopped, chuckling at the memory of the eating contest. "Well, sir, we started in on them hotcakes with plenty of sweetening over them. We got through the first stack together and began on the second. We were eating along at a fast rate and Lomax almost buttered that grasshopper and ate it before he could stop himself. He looked at his plate and got up and left. I finished my second stack of flapjacks, fifty of them, to be exact, and I was declared the winner. Lomax told me later he could eat syrup and butter but not grasshoppers on his hotcakes."

He winked at Rose. "Now that may be true, and it may not," he said. "But it's true I'm a big eater. I'm a singer too."

He began to sing in a pleasant voice:

[ *113* ]

*"I'll eat when I'm hungry,*
*I'll drink when I'm dry,*
*If the devil don't get me,*
*I'll lay down and die.*

*I'll tune up my fiddle,*
*And I'll rosin my bow,*
*I'll make myself welcome*
*Wherever I go."*

Jim jumped to his feet and pretended to play a fiddle, humming the tune loudly. The others clapped their hands in time to the song. He sang faster, sawing on his "fiddle" and hopping around the room.

*"The hardest work I ever did*
*Was a-braking on a train;*
*The easiest work I ever did*
*Was a-hugging Liza Jane.*

*When I went to see her,*
*She met me at the door;*
*Her shoes and stockings in her hand*
*And her feet all over the floor."*

Soon he began to pant. After another verse he stopped. "Don't stop, Jim," cried Mark.

*Jim jumped to his feet and pretended to play a fiddle*

"Well, I had to stop. The strings on the fiddle busted," Jim gasped. While the others laughed, he sat down and wiped his forehead.

"Tell us about when you rode for the Express, Jim," Mark begged. Singing was fine, but he liked stories best.

"Well, I was in San Francisco when the Pony

Express began. I was seeing the town and wondering what I'd try next," Jim told them.

"I had been a prospector, a wagon driver, and a blacksmith's helper. Well, I saw the nankeen-colored pony leave the Alta Telegraph Company in San Fran with the first Express mail. There were big goings-on while that pony trotted to the side-

wheeler boat. Then the boat took the pony and rider by water all the way to Sacramento."

"That's surely boat express and not pony express," Mark said.

"All mail and passengers and freight go by water from San Francisco to Sacramento," Jim replied. "The real beginning of the Pony Express run is, of course, at Sacramento. From there over the Sierra Nevada Mountains is rough going. Warren Upson took the first Pony mail over the Sierras in a snowstorm and it was bad, I hear. He got lost, but he kept going and the mail went through on time."

"Where did your route go?" asked Mr. Claggett.

"I worked out of Carson City," Jim replied. "Sometimes east across the desert, sometimes over the Sierras by Lake Tahoe toward the coast. I had a bad time only once and that was during the Paiute war."

"We know about that war, don't we, Rose?" Mark said to his sister.

"I was a-riding east from Carson City through some rugged country. When I reached a rise on the trail, I saw Indians waiting for me at the bottom," Jim continued.

"I ducked back behind the hill and rode for a

ravine I knew. When I got to it, there were Indians there too. Well, I didn't know what to do for a moment. But I wheeled my horse and headed for another way around the Indians. I passed a clump of greasewood bushes and hid there with the mochila. I sent my horse on. The Indians chased the horse, and when they had gone I hiked the three miles to the next station and rode on. Boy, that was a close shave!"

"I heard that a fellow named Bob Ellison rode two hundred and eighteen miles in fifteen hours," Wilson spoke up. "And one of his ponies carried him over seventy miles at a run. Some horse and some rider, believe me."

Jim nodded. "Bob told me about that," he said. "He reached one station and the rider who was to take his place had quit. The station keeper gave Bob fifty dollars to ride that other man's run. Bob took it and had a rough time of it. He found one station deserted, the man in charge scalped. At another station, the keeper had gone for help, leaving his son in charge. The Paiutes had scalped and killed the boy. But Bob, like all Express riders, got the mail through."

"I don't reckon there has ever been such a heroic group of men as the Pony Express riders,"

Mr. Claggett said. "Danger and blizzards and storms—still they ride on."

"It's a great life all right," Jim said, "if you're not too fat."

Mark sighed. "I sure wish I was old enough," he stated. "There's been plenty of excitement here at this station, but I'd rather ride the mail through than anything."

Wilson looked sober. "It's not all so exciting," he said. "The dangers and hardships a rider goes through aren't always fun. Mostly it's just real hard work."

"I guess so," Mark answered. "But I'd still like to carry the mail and ride for the Express Company."

"Well, you may get a chance someday," Jim told him.

Mark stared into the fire. He could see the rider staggering into the station, wounded by Indian arrows and unable to go on. And *himself*, Mark Claggett, the hostler, seizing the mochila, swinging up on the pony, ready to ride and carry the mail for the Pony Express!

# CHAPTER THIRTEEN

## *The Masked Bandit*

---

BY THE following day the rain had stopped and the sky was clear. Jim Johnston stood in the open door, gazing out. "Well, Mr. Claggett, me and old Wilson had best ride on," he said.

"You're welcome to stay longer," Mr. Claggett told him.

"Please stay another day or so," begged Mark. "We can go hunting and you can sing us some more songs."

"We can't afford to wear out our welcome," Wilson put in. "And Jim's such a big eater, he wears out a welcome pretty fast."

"Well," laughed Jim, "I've found one of the best cooks in the country." He moved to the table and picked up a cold biscuit. "I want to take this to remind me of you, Miss Rose."

He sang:

> "Wish I had a nickel,
> Wish I had a dime,
> Wish I had a pretty li'l gal
> To cook biscuits all the time.
>
> "Oh, biscuits black and biscuits cold,
> I love biscuits one day old.
> I got a cook, her name is Rose,
> Cooks good biscuits for her beaus."

When he finished, he popped the biscuit in his mouth. Rose and Mark giggled together. They hated to see Jim go. Days would never be dull or evenings long with a person like him around.

"Well, I'll tell you I'd stay right here with you," Jim said, "if I didn't have to get back East and enlist in the army."

"The army!" exclaimed Mark in surprise. "You're too easygoing to make a fighter."

"Good or bad, the nation is going to need all the fighters it can get soon," Jim said. "This squabble between the Northern states and the Southern states over slavery and States' Rights has gone on too long. I figure there'll be fighting before it's all over and done with."

Mr. Claggett nodded solemnly. "You're right, Jim," he replied. "These are certainly dangerous times. Of the four men running for President in this 1860 election, only Abraham Lincoln seems to me to be strong enough to keep the Union together."

"Papa heard Lincoln speak several times when we used to live in Illinois," Rose explained.

"Yes, Lincoln's a fine man," Wilson spoke up. "But Jim's right. I don't believe even Lincoln can keep us out of war. People have gotten so bitter over the slavery question, they'll never consent to a peaceful settlement."

The two travelers moved out the door with their saddlebags. They went to the corral and saddled their horses.

"You Claggetts keep the Pony Express running," Jim said as he mounted. "Thanks for your good company and if you ever come out our way, look us up." They waved good-by and rode off.

"We will," Rose called after them.

She waved and then turned to her brother.

"Come and patch your breeches, Mark," she ordered. "My Tuesday sneeze was right and you lost our bet."

Mark groaned. He hadn't thought of that. But the sneeze had been right. Not one but *two* strangers had arrived. With a deep sigh, he picked up the needle and began to sew awkwardly.

November came and the days stayed bright and clear. Mark thought often about the possibility of a war. It made him feel scared and depressed.

Then the Express officials sent a message to all the station keepers to prepare for a fast run. The company wanted the presidential election news to get to California in the fastest time possible. The best ponies were kept from the regular runs and saved for the fast schedule.

"But why is it so important for California to hear about the election?" Rose asked on the morning the fast run was to come through Egan Canyon.

"California is a fairly young state," Mr. Claggett explained. "And it is having a lot of trouble these days over slavery. Although it was admitted to the Union as a non-slave state, many Californians want the state to have slavery. Some people want to divide it up and make it two states. Others

[ *124* ]

think California should leave the Union and become an independent country. Naturally, the outcome of the election is important to a state so upset with plots and counterplots."

"If Mr. Lincoln has been elected, do you think California will stay in the Union?" asked Mark.

"Yes, I do," Mr. Claggett replied. "I think the people there will stand behind Lincoln even if the nation goes to war. But that's all in the future. Now we've been put on our honor to help get the news through. We don't want another failure here at Egan Station." He sighed.

Rose looked worried. Life was certainly complicated with wars and elections and lost letters. She'd bake a cake. That might make them all feel better.

She turned to Mark. "Get me some more wood, Mark," she begged.

"You'll have to wait," Mark replied. "I've got to clean out the horse shed and feed the ponies."

"You're the worst brother I've got," Rose exclaimed. "And you think more of those ponies than you do of me." She flounced out the door indignantly.

Mark followed her out and turned toward the corral. He stood there while Four Boots came up to the fence to be petted. "If we were any good, boy," he told the pony, "we'd be on that fast run today."

Suddenly he felt something press into his back. "Tie those four ponies together and bring them here," a voice commanded.

Mark was shoved right into the corral. "Don't yell or your pa will see daylight through a hole I'll shoot in your head," the voice growled.

Mark caught the ponies with a few minutes' work. He kept glancing at the bandit, who wore a black hat with a black handkerchief over the lower part of his face. Those eyes looked like killer's eyes all right, Mark decided, and he did everything he was told.

But his heart was heavy. If this robber went off with the ponies, Egan Canyon Station could chalk up another black mark against itself. The Pony rider would have to use the same animal on to Ruby Valley and that would certainly slow down his time—when they were trying for a record!

Mark wished desperately that he could do something. But that gun shining in the morning sun was pointed right at him.

The bandit followed Mark inside the station. Mr. Claggett was taken by surprise. The bandit forced him to get together all his money and his watch, all the guns and ammunition in the station.

The masked man put it all in a sack. Throwing it over his shoulder, he backed toward the door. He kept Mark and Mr. Claggett covered with his revolver.

*The bandit followed Mark inside the station*

The bandit stopped in the doorway. "You've been so obliging," he sneered, "maybe I'll pay you another visit sometime."

He stepped backward through the station door.

# CHAPTER FOURTEEN

## *Rose to the Rescue*

---

ROSE paused by the woodpile behind the station, breathing the pine-fragrant air. She looked off at the distant blue mountains. She thought about how much she had come to like her life here. It wasn't so lonely with the riders and supply wagons coming and going.

And the countryside, which had seemed so strange at first, now seemed beautiful. It would be perfect for all of them here if it weren't for the trouble caused by the missing letter.

A mule deer drifted out of the woods and across the meadow. Rose laughed at its ridiculous-looking ears. Beyond the woodpile she spied a patch of late-blooming meadow rue.

"I'll have to come back and pick those flowers

this afternoon," she reminded herself. "Flowers on a table make a meal cheerful and Papa needs cheering."

She gathered an armload of wood and returned to the station. As she turned the corner of the building, she saw the strange horse by the doorway. Beyond it stood the Express ponies, roped together. Their lead line was tied to the saddle horn of the strange horse.

She stopped. What was going on? Through the open door she heard a harsh voice command her father to put all the guns and ammunition in a sack.

A bandit!

Her heart leaped up into her throat and she all but dropped the load of wood. Her father and brother would be shot while she hid outside. She must do something—but what could she do against an armed robber?

She quietly placed the wood on the ground. "I might sneak up and lead off the horses," she thought.

The ponies were very important today. She ought to save them. But she decided against that. The bandit would hear the horses leaving and shoot her. She shuddered, picturing in her mind how she'd look lying on the ground all bloody and as full of bullet holes as a sieve.

Now she heard the bandit backing toward the door. She looked around desperately. What could she do?

Her eyes fell on the wood. She picked up a piece of it. Tiptoeing along the wall, she stopped by the doorway.

The bandit stood there with his back to her and with the revolver in his left hand. "Maybe I'll pay you another visit sometime," he said, and backed outside.

Rose raised the stick and with all her might brought it down on the bandit's hand holding the gun. The revolver fell to the floor of the station with a loud clatter.

"Papa!" she screamed. "Get the gun!"

The bandit dropped the bag of loot and jumped for his horse.

"Stop where you are or I'll pump you full of your own lead," Mr. Claggett shouted. He rushed from the station with the bandit's gun in his hand.

The bandit stopped and stood facing them, rubbing his hand where Rose had hit him.

"Get a rope, Mark," Mr. Claggett ordered. Without taking his eyes from the stranger, he said

*The bandit stood there with his back to Rose*

to Rose, "That was quick thinking, Rose. You're going to be a Wild West girl yet."

Rose felt so weak, she leaned against the rock wall. Her heart just wouldn't slow down.

"I didn't—didn't break his hand, did I?" she asked. "I didn't mean to hit him so hard."

Mark came out with the rope. "Aw, Rose, you're the worst," he remarked. "If you do anything worth doing, you start being wishy-washy and worrying about hurting somebody."

He tied the man's hands and feet and jerked off the mask. It was a cruel face with a red scar beside the mouth. The man was a complete stranger to the Claggetts.

"I—I—" Rose began, staring at the man.

Mark took her by the shoulders and marched her inside the station. "No apologizing to bandits," he laughed. "He didn't come to pay a sociable visit and eat your cake and drink your tea, Miss Tender Heart."

Mark pushed his sister gently down into a chair. "Now you sit there and I will cook the breakfast," he told her. "You deserve something for your bravery."

"But what about the bandit?" asked Rose.

[ *134* ]

"I will ride to Ruby Valley for help," Mark told her. "Let's have some breakfast first."

After the meal Mark saddled Four Boots and rode to Ruby Valley. He hated to miss seeing the arrival of the Express rider with the election news. But none of the Claggetts liked having a robber tied up in the corral.

At Ruby Valley Station Mark explained what had happened. Two men from the station returned with him.

"Egan Canyon has certainly had its share of troubles," one of the men said as they rode along. "Did you ever find what happened to that letter that got lost?"

"No," Mark answered sadly. "My father is still on probation. And it does seem as though luck were against us. When this horse thief almost got away with the ponies, my heart sank. I knew if he did, the Express rider wouldn't have a fresh mount, he'd be slowed down, and Egan Station would have failed again."

"Well, cheer up," the man said. "It didn't happen. And here comes the rider now."

The rider rode past them at a gallop.

"Who won?" they shouted.

"Lincoln!" The wind tore the word from the rider's lips.

"Lincoln!" the second man said. "That means war surely. But I believe California will stick with the Union and Lincoln. And that's important."

War! Mark felt a little shiver go up and down his spine. What would the coming months bring to the Claggetts, the Pony Express, and the nation?

# CHAPTER FIFTEEN

## *Mark Carries the Mail*

---

THE Claggetts learned later that the election news had been carried by the Pony Express in eight days. The rider had picked up the presidential results at St. Joseph, Missouri. Then the news was carried by Pony to Fort Churchill, Nevada. Here the telegraph operator sent the news by wire to California.

The months passed and the new year of 1861 came. The Claggetts went about their Express duties as usual through the cold winter months. Cyrus Platt occasionally brought them newspapers, and the slow-moving winter days were spent discussing the news.

"The papers report that Californians are having a difficult time," Mr. Claggett told his children.

"A group called the Knights of the Golden Circle are trying to make an independent nation of California and the rest of the Pacific Coast."

"What about back East?" Mark asked. "Do people say war is coming?"

Mr. Claggett nodded soberly. "Most of the editors think war became unavoidable when South Carolina seceded from the Union in December," he told Mark.

"With one state out, four or five others are sure to follow. And some of the border states say that if the national government makes war on the South they will stand by the slaveholding Confederacy."

He pursed his lips and went on sadly. "While he was in office President Buchanan did nothing to the rebels trying to break up the Union. And war is coming now unless Abraham Lincoln in his Inaugural Address on March 4th has some definite plan to preserve the Union and keep us from civil war. You know Abe once said in a speech that 'a house divided against itself cannot stand.' "

Mr. Claggett looked into the fire a moment. Then he turned back and spoke, "Lincoln believes in the states staying united, and I wouldn't be surprised if his speech in March was rushed by Pony from Fort Kearny to the next telegraph station. It's a sixteen-hundred-mile run to Fort Churchill, but I bet they'll try it, and wire the speech from there to California. Mr. Lincoln will need California's gold if war does come. Certainly, strong words from him might keep California from seceding and the people there from fighting each other."

Mr. Claggett prophesied correctly. The Pony Express prepared to rush the President's Inaugural Address to California in fast time.

The day the Express carrying Lincoln's speech was due, Mark saddled the fastest pony and had it waiting. It was a dark, chill day. Snow fell and the wind blew all afternoon. By dark a real blizzard was howling around the stationhouse.

"There won't be any fast time made on *this* run," Mr. Claggett observed. "In fact, I'll be surprised if the Pony rider gets through this snowstorm at all."

He stood with his back to the fire, warming his hands. "I've never seen such a blizzard in my life."

The three sat close to the fire, worried about the Pony rider. Mr. Claggett felt sure something had happened and wondered whether to go out looking for him.

[ *139* ]

"It wouldn't do much good," Mark said. "You couldn't see five feet ahead in this snowstorm."

"Don't do it, Papa," begged Rose.

"I guess you're right, but I'm worried just the same," Mr. Claggett said.

Rose sighed. "Oh, I do hope he's all right," she remarked anxiously. "And oh, I feel so sorry for the poor ponies out there in the snow."

"You're a kind-hearted child, Rose," Mr. Claggett told her. "But these ponies are tough and are used to bad weather. They are protected by the shed, and Mark and I put down hay for them to lie in and keep warm."

They sat in silence then, listening for any sound or cry the rider might give. By nine o'clock Rose was too sleepy to wait up any longer. She went to bed.

Mark hated to go to bed, though he was sleepy too. He believed Cyrus Platt would get through, even if he was late.

Mark shivered, as he thought how cold and terrible it must be coming up Egan Canyon through the blizzard on a pony. It made him appreciate the bright warmth of the fire.

He got up and threw another pine log on the hearth. Mr. Claggett nodded in his chair, his head sinking lower and lower on his chest. Mark settled down in the other chair beside his father.

The wind blew down the chimney and smoke billowed out into the room. A spark popped out and Mark stepped on it.

He waited a short while longer, then he lay down on his bed in his clothes. He pulled a blanket over him and went to sleep.

It was several hours later when Mark awoke with a start and sat up. There was a faint sound at the door.

"What's that?" Mark asked, springing to his feet.

Again there was the same noise.

"Papa, something's scratching at the door," Mark said, shaking his father's shoulder.

Mr. Claggett followed his son. Mark threw open the door. A pony stood there in the snow. On the doorstep lay a dark figure.

"It's Cyrus Platt!" cried Mark.

They dragged him inside and laid him on Mark's bed. Rose got up to help them tend the rider. Both his hands and feet were frozen. He could hardly talk, he was so exhausted by his ride through the blizzard.

"He can't go on," Mr. Claggett said. "More exposure would kill him. I'm afraid Lincoln's speech will have to wait here till this storm dies away."

Mark got up from beside Platt. "No," he said. "We can't fail the Pony Express. I'll carry it! I know the route to Ruby Valley."

# CHAPTER SIXTEEN

## *The Blizzard*

---

MARK began to put on the warmest clothes he had. As he pulled heavy woolen socks on his feet, he paused.

Outside, the wind beat against the stationhouse with fury. Sleet rattled coldly against the door. Mark bit his lip anxiously. Was he doing a foolish thing by going out in this blizzard?

No, somebody had to carry the President's Inaugural Address. He was the only one here who could.

He looked up to find his sister's eyes on him. She looked frightened. He winked and slipped quickly into his boots.

"Is that hot tea ready, Rose?" he asked. "Cyrus

said tea is better than coffee to keep you going. And us Pony Express riders need to keep alert."

He smiled to himself as he said it. "Pony Express rider." He swelled with pride. He was one at last. He'd better get going. He took the canteen of hot tea his sister gave him.

"Are you going to ride the pony we have saddled?" Mr. Claggett asked. He was sitting beside Platt, feeding him hot tea in a spoon. The Pony rider's white face and hollow eyes turned toward Mark.

With an effort, Platt spoke. "Mark, ride a pony who trusts you, so you can trust it," he said.

Mark nodded. It wouldn't do to be out in this blizzard with a rambunctious, biting pony of which he was half afraid. "I'll ride Four Boots," he decided. "Speed is impossible in this heavy snow. Four Boots' bullet wound won't bother him. He'll get me to Ruby Valley."

Mr. Claggett agreed. "I'll saddle for you and let you stay by the fire as long as you can," he said.

He started for the door and stopped. He turned and looked at his son. "Mark, I hate to let you go out in this blizzard," he said in a low voice. "I'm too heavy to go myself. The Express pony stands a better chance of getting through with a light rider.

But it's too dangerous for you. I have a mind not to let you go."

He looked at Mark a long moment. Mark knew what he was thinking. The Inaugural Address would stop at Egan Canyon Station. That would be another black mark!

"I'll be all right, Papa," Mark said quickly.

Mr. Claggett nodded. He turned and went out to the corral. A few minutes later he was at the front door with Four Boots. The light Express saddle and the mochila were on the sorrel.

Mark told Rose and his father and Cyrus Platt good-by and got into the saddle. "Don't worry," he called as he rode away. "I'll make it all right."

He left the station with a light heart. The snow pelted his face, but it was letting up. He was not cold and Four Boots was making good headway down the mountain. The wind was sharp at times, but nothing to worry about, that he could see. This was going to be easy even in the dark, he told himself.

He kept Four Boots going at a trot through the pines and rocks. Then he reached an unprotected spot and the wind beat at him with full force. Its cold cut through his clothes so that he began to shiver in spite of himself.

[ *145* ]

Battling the wind, Four Boots slowed to a walk. The snow fell more swiftly. It slapped Mark in the face with such force that he could hardly breathe.

He ducked his head, grimacing at the chill that went through him.

The pony took a few more steps and stopped. "Go on, Four Boots," Mark urged. "We can't stop here." He patted the animal's head.

Four Boots went on with a snort. The snow fell more thickly. Mark let the reins drop. It was up to Four Boots now to keep to the trail.

Mark trusted the sorrel. He leaned forward and again patted his neck. "All right, boy, keep going."

On they went through the blizzard. Ice formed around Mark's nose and mouth. His ears felt like blocks of ice. His legs were so cold, he had no feeling in them. He kept beating them with his hands. He didn't want his feet to freeze like Cyrus Platt's.

Four Boots slid floundering from the trail. The snow came up to the stirrups. Mark got the mustang turned around and back to the spot where they had left the trail.

Again he urged Four Boots on. The horse went first this way and then that. Once he backed up, striking off in a direction Mark knew must be wrong. Finally the pony stopped altogether. What was the matter with Four Boots?

Mark got down and moved forward. There was a tree lying in their way. He felt his way around, leading the pony. Then he mounted and went on. He wished daylight would come so he could hunt for a familiar landmark.

The wind died away and then roared back. Mark flinched as it lashed at him. His face stung from the snow and ice. His body quivered. It was more than he could stand. He had never felt such a wind.

He leaned out of the saddle, peering intently into the snow. He brushed against a rock and his head hit an icicle. A piece of it fell off on him, scaring the pony.

Mark stretched out his arm and touched the rock. He put out his other arm. There was a rock there too. Now he knew they were off the trail. Their way to Ruby Valley did not lead through a canyon as narrow as this one he had discovered.

"We're lost, Four Boots." He spoke aloud, and saying it, he felt a cold, paralyzing fear well up in his throat. Lost! Oh, why hadn't he paid more attention to where he was going!

He stopped short. There was no reason for him to blame himself. He'd done his best in the dark. He would go on, lost or not. He was trying. What more could be expected of him? He was doing his very best to keep Lincoln's speech moving to California. That was all any Express rider could do. And he was now a Pony rider.

"Get going, Four Boots," he said, slapping the pony on the flank.

Four Boots went bravely on, bucking the wind. Ice hung from his muzzle. He shook his head and mane often, trying to shake off the snow.

Then the wind whistled off over the mountains, but the snow still fell. It was quiet, and Mark could hear the pony's heavy breathing.

Between pines and across a frozen stream they went. The land sloped downward here, and Mark felt relieved. At least he was getting off Egan Mountain.

From away off he heard the roar of the wind. Again he flinched as it howled down on him. The cold was intense now. He hunched down into his clothes, trying to keep the snow from sliding down his neck and the wind from cutting his face.

Suddenly Four Boots stopped again. "Go on," Mark shouted impatiently. The pony refused to move. Mark kicked him hard in the ribs. Four Boots did not budge.

Mark climbed laboriously down. What was the matter this time, he asked himself.

"We got to keep moving, Four Boots," Mark said. "I'll lead and you just follow along."

He pulled the reins over the animal's head. His hands were stiff with cold in spite of the woolen mittens he wore. He took the lines and started onward with head bowed against the blinding snow.

He stepped forward and his foot went down, down. He tried to catch himself, but it was too late. He was falling!

[ *149* ]

# CHAPTER SEVENTEEN

## *Behind the Black Rock*

---

WITH a gasp Mark plunged down into darkness and space. His hand still grasped the reins. The leather lines brought him up short with a terrific jerk. Mark dangled against a cliff side. The cutting wind tore at him and banged him against the rock.

Then he felt the lines slipping through his hands. With his mittens on, he was unable to get a firm grip. He grasped the reins as tightly as he could, but his fingers were stiff with cold.

He slipped a little farther down. He tried to dig his toes into the cliff, but it was icy and his booted feet could not find a toehold.

Again he felt himself sliding slowly down. He closed his eyes, sick with fear. His hands reached

*He felt the lines slipping through his hands*

the knotted end of the reins, and he held on there.

But how long could he hope to hold?

Already his arms were aching and cramped with the strain. And would the bridle slip over Four Boots' head? It certainly would, if the pony lowered his head, Mark knew. Four Boots might do just that to keep from being pulled over the cliff by Mark's weight.

There was a rift in the falling snow, and Mark clearly saw Four Boots above him. The mustang stood with stiff neck and rigid forelegs. Mark saw the flaring nostrils and the white puff of the pony's breath. Then the thick snowflakes cut off his vision.

"Back up, Four Boots," Mark said aloud, although he knew the sorrel could not hear him above the now howling wind. "Back up and pull, pull!" he begged.

Mark realized he couldn't hold on much longer. He had no feeling in his hands and arms. Fear clutched at his stomach. He couldn't last.

Then suddenly he felt himself rising. His head came up level with the edge of the cliff. He could see Four Boots braced and straining every muscle. The little horse moved slowly, carefully backward, pulling Mark up.

Mark felt for a foothold to help out, but it was useless. Bit by bit he rose. Then Four Boots slipped. Mark's heart stopped, and he closed his eyes.

He was falling again!

But the mustang regained his footing, and once again the boy moved toward safety. Mark's head, his shoulders were raised above the edge. And now only his legs were dangling over. Still Four Boots backed. At last Mark turned loose the reins and lay exhausted on the ice.

The pony nuzzled at him. His breath was hot on Mark's face. The boy got to his feet and grabbed the mustang around the neck.

"Oh, Four Boots!" he exclaimed. "You've saved my life." He hugged the horse until Four Boots snorted.

Mark threw the reins over the pony's neck. He put his foot in the stirrup and climbed wearily up into the saddle. The mochila was still in place. He wheeled the mustang around and started off again.

"The next time you stop," Mark told the pony, "I'll believe you and not go on."

On through the storm they went. Mark didn't know how much time had passed. It might have been for only a little while or it might have been for hours. He knew nothing but snow and wind and cold. But it seemed to him to be getting lighter.

Sometimes it seemed Four Boots was picking his way down the mountain. And again Mark was sure they went up. But they kept going and that was important. To stop in this blizzard out in the open was to freeze to death.

The storm was blowing itself out. The wind was not nearly as strong as it had been. And when Mark looked around now, he could see a good distance through the snow.

It was early morning. But he did not know where he was.

He was almost exhausted. He nodded, finally dozing off entirely. He awoke to find himself falling from the saddle. He clutched at the saddle horn wildly and stayed on the mustang.

"I'll have to stay awake, or I'll never make it with the speech," he told himself. He knew that drowsiness was one of the first signs of freezing. He shook his head and rubbed his eyes.

The pony plodded wearily on. Again Mark found himself going to sleep.

"This won't do," he muttered fearfully. "I've got to stay awake some way."

He decided to sing. He recalled one of the tunes Jim Johnston had sung at the station about a couple crossing the plains to California. It was called "Sweet Betsy from Pike." The first verse was the only one to which Mark could remember the words.

*"Did you ever hear tell of Sweet Betsy from Pike,*
*Who crossed the wide prairies with her lover Ike,*
*With two yoke of cattle and one spotted hog,*
*A tall Shanghai rooster and an old yeller dog?"*

Mark sang this verse over and over. When he was tired of doing that, he hummed, beating time on the mochila with his hand.

He tried to think of another song to sing, but he could remember neither the words nor the tune of any other.

"I'm too cold to think," he told Four Boots.

So he sang "Sweet Betsy from Pike" on and on. Once Four Boots stopped and turned his head to look at the boy.

"I know I don't sing good," Mark told his pony. "I couldn't carry a tune if it had handles on it. But this is the only way I can keep awake."

Four Boots moved off and kept going steadily. The snow had almost stopped. Mark turned in the saddle and glanced around the mountainside.

It must be after seven o'clock, he figured. The light was pale, for the clouds were thick. But he could see all around him.

A cliff towered sheer and cold looking to one side of him. On the other side was a jumble of snow-covered rocks. Here and there a slender pinnacle rose above the rest. Beyond he looked down on pines, their branches bent and broken by the weight of snow and ice.

There was not a single landmark he recognized. But if he could reach the bottom of the mountain, he believed he might be able to find his way on to Ruby Valley.

He urged Four Boots on, letting the tired pony pick his way among the rocks. He kept the cliff to his right.

The cold was intense. "It wasn't this sharp when the wind blew," Mark complained.

He rubbed his arms and legs and beat at his body to keep warm. He wondered if the temperature was dropping. He and the pony must stop and rest somewhere. But stopping might mean freezing to death.

He yawned. Another minute and he'd be asleep. He decided he'd get off and walk, now that he could see where he was going. That would keep him awake.

He stumbled along beside Four Boots. With a sudden whistle the wind rushed down on him again. A flurry of snow flung itself in his face.

A tall, odd-looking boulder was just ahead. Mark pushed toward it. It would at least shelter them from the wind.

He reached the boulder at last and stood shivering. He couldn't stand this cold much longer. He turned his back to the boulder.

What was that in the cliff wall right ahead? Could it be a cave? Mark's hopes rose. He ran forward. It *was* a cave, and a good big one. Here was shelter, a place to rest awhile.

He went inside the cave, leading Four Boots. A short distance from the entrance he dropped down wearily. For a minute he sat with his head resting on his raised knees. He'd never been so tired and sleepy in his life.

"Well, Wilson Thomas was right," he sighed. "A Pony Express rider does not always have fun." He remembered sitting in front of the station-house fire with plenty of Rose's biscuits inside him. At that time Mark hadn't really believed Wilson. He knew better now.

He raised his head. His pony stood before him with his head hanging wearily down and his feet spread wide. He seemed ready to drop from exhaustion, Mark thought.

"Poor Four Boots," Mark said soothingly. "You've really had a rough time today. I wish I had some corn for you."

After the wind and cold outside, the cave seemed warm and comfortable. Mark was even sleepier than he'd been while riding.

"I'd better drink my tea," he thought.

Mark got up and went to the pony. He patted Four Boots' flank as he took the canteen strap from over the saddle horn.

Sitting down, Mark took a drink of the cold, sweet tea. It tasted good, and he finished the canteen. He felt refreshed and wide awake now.

He glanced outside. The snow still fell. But the worst of the blizzard was over, Mark believed. As soon as possible, he should get started.

He looked back to Four Boots. Was the pony rested enough to go on now? He would like to stay here long enough to be sure Four Boots had recovered his strength.

But he had to get on with Lincoln's Address. It

had to get through, no matter what condition the mustang was in.

Mark had heard plenty of stories of men riding their horses until they dropped dead. It would break his heart if anything happened to Four Boots. Nevertheless he got to his feet and picked up the reins. "We've got to go, Four Boots," he said. "Ready or not, we've got to go on."

Four Boots wiggled his ears forward. He nuzzled at the boy's hand. Mark rubbed the velvety nostrils. The pony nickered and tossed his mane.

As Mark moved through the dim cave, he stumbled over something. It hit the floor with a clang of metal.

"What's that?" he asked. He bent over and in-spected the object.

"An iron pot!" he exclaimed in surprise. "What in the world is it doing here?"

For the first time he looked around the cave. There were drawings on the walls—Indian paint-ings! Indians! This was an Indian cave, but he didn't believe Indians lived here. He was still safe.

He examined the metal pot and found pieces of something soft clinging to the bottom. He took a piece to the cave entrance where the light was bet-ter. It was some kind of soft metal. He scratched it with his thumbnail.

It was gold!

# CHAPTER EIGHTEEN

## *Home Again*

---

W HY," Mark exclaimed aloud, "this must be the Indian gold mine Papa found!"

He tingled with excitement. What had Papa said—a cave with a tall, black rock standing in front of it?

Mark rushed out of the cave. There was the boulder he had sheltered against when he first saw the cave. It was nearly twenty feet tall and black as coal.

"I should have recognized it earlier," he thought. "But I was thinking about saving my life, not finding gold."

The Express! Right now he should be thinking about getting the Inaugural Address to Ruby Valley. He was an Express rider, not a gold miner.

He ran back into the cave and led Four Boots

out into the open. Hastily he checked the saddle, then threw himself on the pony's back. He was lost. It might take him some time to find the way. He mustn't lose any more time.

The sun had not broken through the heavy gray clouds. But the snow had stopped, and the white blanket on the ground reflected and magnified the light. Mark could see perfectly, yet nothing looked familiar.

He dug his heels into Four Boots' sides. They moved on along the cliff wall. Mark would have liked to take time to explore his surroundings, so that he would be able to recognize the way to the cave when he returned. But he *had* to hurry on.

Mark guided the horse between two rocks. Now the ground fell rapidly away beneath them. "At least we're getting off the mountain," Mark thought. The way was steep and rough, and Four Boots slid a great deal, but in a short while they were down.

Mark looked all around. Just where were they? He glanced back the way they had come. There wasn't a sign of the black rock or of the cave.

But a few hundred yards south of him, a huge craggy rock, split at the top, stuck up out of the snow.

"That's it!" he shouted happily. "That's the big rock on the trail to Ruby Valley where the road comes down off the mountain. I know where we are now."

He headed Four Boots west across the snow-covered stretch of desert. As he rode along, Mark realized he had forgotten his tiredness and sleepiness. Even Four Boots seemed refreshed and ready for anything.

The boy whistled and sang and talked to himself. "I'm a real Express rider," he shouted happily. "I can ride the mail through a blizzard and find a gold mine at the same time. Whooopeee! I'm the toughest critter between here and the western ocean."

Four Boots went steadily on. By the time the station at Ruby Valley came into sight, however, Mark was mighty glad to see it. The cold, the hours of hard riding, the lack of food and sleep, were telling on him. And Four Boots was almost exhausted, his steps were getting slower and slower.

The door of the station swung open, and a man's head stuck out. "Mail-o!" he shouted.

Several men ran from the station to stare at Mark. The boy drew himself up, sitting erect on Four Boots.

[ *163* ]

"It's Claggett's boy!" someone shouted in amazement.

"Where's Platt?" asked a second man.

"How in the world did you get through that blizzard?"

"Worst blizzard I've ever seen," a tall man remarked, helping Mark from his pony. "How on earth did you do it, son?"

"Aw, it wasn't so bad," Mark said modestly.

"Don't tell me it wasn't bad," the tall man answered. "It was terrible."

Mark grinned at the men around him. "I was scared," he owned up. "But Platt had frozen his hands and feet, and somebody had to get Lincoln's speech through. There was only me, and I'm sure glad this is all over with."

"Boy, you got plenty of spunk," a man with a beard said. He stepped up to Mark and held out his hand. "I want to shake your hand, by gum."

The men crowded close, shaking Mark's hand and pounding him on the back and telling him what a great thing it was he'd done. He stood there with the mochila in his hands, feeling sheepish at the reception.

"Here comes Ferris, the next rider," someone shouted.

A small, wiry fellow stepped up to Mark. "Howdy, Claggett," he said. "How does it feel to be a Pony rider?"

"Fine," answered Mark, handing him the mochila.

Ferris took the leather mail pouch and put it on his pony. "You'll have to tell me your adventures sometime," he said. He mounted and trotted away. "Take care of him, boys, he's a good man to have carrying the mail!"

[ *165* ]

Mark stumbled into the station. He was almost asleep on his feet. But he turned back. "My horse —Four Boots," he mumbled.

"Your pony's already being taken care of," someone said.

"Thanks. It was really Four Boots who got through the storm," Mark spoke sleepily. He fell on the bed and was asleep almost at once.

Hours later he awoke, feeling rested and hungry. Somebody had taken off his wet boots and his jacket without Mark even knowing it. He threw back the blankets.

"Where can a feller get something to eat around here?" he asked.

A fat man brought him a cup of coffee, a bowl of stew, and a big hunk of bread. Mark ate it and had second helpings of everything.

When he finished, he went to the door and looked out. It was growing dark. "Heck!" he exclaimed. "I can't get back now. I'll have to wait till morning."

"You may have to wait longer than that," the fat man said. "You ain't really fit to travel yet."

Mark groaned to himself. He'd never be able to wait. Rose and his father would be worried about him. And he had such a heap of good news to tell

[ *166* ]

them. He went and sat by the fire. At least he could enjoy being warm and fed and comfortable.

In a few minutes he was surprised to find himself growing sleepy again. The fat man had been right. He wasn't yet ready to make the trip home. He got back into bed and went to sleep.

By noon the next day Mark was able to leave Ruby Valley Station. He left Four Boots behind to get a longer rest. The doctor rode with him to see Cyrus Platt. The wind and sun had almost cleared the trail. In a short time the two riders came in sight of Egan Canyon Station.

Mark galloped ahead. He jumped from his pony and ran into the hut.

"Mark!" cried Rose, dropping a pan with a clatter. She threw her arms around him. Then she drew away and picked up the pan. "I declare, Mark Claggett, you're more trouble than you're worth," she said crossly. "I'm always giving you up for dead and then you turn up like a bad penny."

Mr. Claggett laughed. "She doesn't mean it, Mark," he said. "She's been so worried, she couldn't eat. And I don't mind telling you I'm *certainly* glad to see you home safe."

Mark grinned and gave Rose a big hug. "Never mind, sister," he told her. "I know you're jealous because you didn't get to make the ride. But I'll let you polish all my medals as soon as the Express Company gives them to me!"

"So you rode the mail!" Cyrus Platt spoke up. Mark had not noticed him sitting by the fire. The rider smiled at Mark. "Through a blizzard too. You're a good boy, Mark, and I'd like to shake hands with you, but my fingers are pretty sore still."

"I'm sorry to hear that," Mark said. "But I brought the doctor with me. Here he is."

The doctor examined Cyrus' hands and feet. "You're a good nurse, Miss Rose," he said. "This boy's in fine shape. In fact, I think he'll be able to ride back with me in the morning."

"Well, now, Mark, tell us all about it," Mr. Claggett commanded. "Cyrus and Rose and I are anxious to hear just what happened to you."

So Mark told all about the hard ride and Four Boots saving his life and the long hours in the snow. When he came to the cave, he hesitated.

Mark wanted to tell Mr. Claggett and Rose about his discovery, but he thought it best to wait till Platt and the doctor left. He trusted both of the visitors. Yet he knew it might be some time before

[ *168* ]

he and his father would be able to get out and re-
locate the mine and stake a claim.

The fewer people who knew about it, the better.
Cyrus or the doctor might accidentally say some-

thing about it in Ruby Valley. And Mark knew
there were always unscrupulous men who wouldn't
hesitate to follow up the hint and try to find the
mine for themselves.

No, it was best to wait with the news. He squirmed with impatience. How could he wait till Platt and the doctor had gone?

But he skipped the part about the cave and told about his pony. "It was really Four Boots who got through," he finished. "I'd have died without him."

"I'll bake Four Boots a cake," Rose promised.

After supper there was more talk about blizzards and riders being lost. Mark almost told about the gold mine once, but caught himself just in time.

At last it was bedtime. Mark lay on a pallet on the floor so that Cyrus might keep his bed. He ached with impatience for morning to come, and he just couldn't go to sleep. He was too excited. He twisted and squirmed.

"Go to sleep!" Rose hissed.

He lay still then, staring at the fire. And after a while he fell asleep.

# CHAPTER NINETEEN

## *The Lost Letter*

---

THE next morning dawned bright and warm.

"It's a real spring day," Rose said, throwing open the door of the station.

"That's fine," said the doctor. "I want good weather if Cyrus is going out in it." He yawned and stretched. "It makes me feel lazy, though. I guess there's no reason to hurry back to Ruby Valley."

No hurry! Mark was wild to see the last of them. Cyrus was the best friend he had, and he liked the doctor. But, oh, how he wished he could hurry them off to Ruby Valley so he could tell his father and sister his news.

"It's so warm, it may rain," he said as casually as he could. "The last time we had clouds like that to the south, it rained."

"Well, we'd best leave now," the doctor decided. "I don't want Cyrus to get caught in a rain."

As soon as the doctor and Cyrus had ridden off, Mark hurried Rose and his father into the station. In a few minutes he had told them his good news.

"Yes, you're right!" exclaimed Mr. Claggett. "I remember now. I went up the mountain from the Ruby Valley side and came on the cave. It was north of the trail. If it doesn't storm this afternoon, I'll ride over there and stake my claim."

Mr. Claggett did, and returned late that night. Rose and Mark were waiting for him. "Yes, it is the mine I found, and it's a good one," he told the two children. "I'll have samples assayed right away."

"Will we be rich?" asked Rose.

Her father smiled. "If I can get enough money out of it to pay Norris for his business loss, I'll be satisfied," he answered. "It's bad enough to have Mr. Ficklin accuse me of carelessness without being responsible for Mr. Norris's bad deal."

"Will you stay here and work the mine?" asked Mark.

"I don't know," Mr. Claggett said thoughtfully. "I'll have to think it over."

"What about the Indians?" Rose asked. "Is it really their mine?"

[ *172* ]

"No," answered Mr. Claggett. "Since the Paiute war, the Indians of Nevada have all been placed on what is to be a reservation around Pyramid Lake, and this country is open for settlement and mining."

Mr. Claggett filed his claims later. The assayed samples showed the mine to be a rich one.

This was wonderful news for the Claggetts. But there was bad news at this time, too. War had been declared between the Union and the states which had seceded. California did not secede.

"The Pony Express can take some credit for that," Mr. Claggett said. "We helped to keep California in close touch with the East and made her feel a real part of the Union. Her loyalty and her gold will help the states become a real Union once more."

"Do you think the war will last long, Papa?" asked Mark.

"I'm afraid it will," Mr. Claggett answered sadly.

"I guess the Pony Express will be needed to carry messages and important news to California," Rose said.

"For a while it will," Mr Claggett replied. "But you know telegraph wires have already been

[ *173* ]

strung across a good part of the continent. Now that war has been declared, every effort will be made to complete the line from coast to coast.

"It may not be possible to do it. But if it is, wires and poles will carry the messages over mountain passes and deserts, rather than sturdy mustangs and brave boys."

"Well, what will we do if the Pony Express closes up?" Mark wanted to know.

"I've made up my mind to sell the gold mine," Mr. Claggett told him. "Then I think we'll buy a farm in California. I want to go back to farming, and California is wonderful country. Besides you two have been alone out in the desert long enough. I want you to be close to a town where you can go to school and meet other young people."

Rose looked pleased. Mark was glad, too, in a way. But he would hate to say good-by to the Pony Express, the wiry little ponies, and the fine young men who rode them.

"At least, I got to ride the mail," he said proudly to himself. "And in spite of the blizzards we carried the President's Address in twelve days!"

The spring and summer days of 1861 went by. War was raging fiercely in the East and every newspaper brought sad news. It also told that the two ends of the telegraph line—one from the East, one from the West—were rapidly drawing closer together.

One day the mail brought a letter to Mr. Claggett. It was from a gold-mining company in California. The company wanted to buy the mine and

[ *175* ]

offered a good price for it. Mr. Claggett decided to accept.

"Will we leave for California right away?" Mark inquired.

"No," Mr. Claggett answered. "I'll stay till the last pony makes its last ride."

"Those are kind words," said a voice at the open door. "Mr. Claggett, I always knew you were a loyal employee. Not many men would stay in this lonely station when they had money enough to get away from it."

"Papa, it's Mr. Ficklin," cried Rose. "Come in, sir."

"Thank you, I will," the superintendent answered. "I'm making the rounds to tell all the Express Company employees good-by and thank them for their good work. As you know, in a few weeks the telegraph lines will be completed, and the usefulness of the Pony Express will be over. And I've come to express the company's gratitude to those who stuck with us through Indian raids and blizzards and all our other troubles."

"We'll be sorry to see the last of the Pony Express," said Mr. Claggett. "The Express was a wonderful thing."

Mr. Ficklin nodded. "The Express has never

[ *176* ]

made money for its owners," he told them. "But it did the people of this nation a very great service. I don't think this country will ever forget the Pony Express."

"I'm glad I got to ride the mail that time," Mark murmured.

"I'm glad too," Mr. Ficklin agreed. "You're a good boy and I'm happy that you Claggetts have had such a fine piece of luck. I heard about your mine." He turned to Rose. "I guess living out here has been hard on you, Miss Rose. I know you'll be glad to get back to town."

"Well," Rose smiled, "I liked Egan Canyon and being a help to the Pony Express. But I will like going to church and shopping in stores again. And I need to buy some new clothes. I've outgrown all my nice things. And of course I never had a chance to wear them out here."

"I bet she's even outgrown her parasol," Mark laughed. "Or she's forgotten how to carry it and twirl it dainty-like over her shoulder."

"No, I haven't," Rose cried. With a swirl of skirts she turned and pulled the valise from its hiding place. Quickly she opened it and drew out the parasol. She popped the silk parasol open and tipped it over her shoulder.

[ *177* ]

"There," she exclaimed and minced across the room.

"Wait, you dropped something out of the parasol," Mark said. He stooped and picked it up. "It's

a letter, addressed to Mr. Theo Norris, in care of the Lanscor Campany, San Francisco."

There was a moment's stunned silence in the

room. "The *letter*," breathed Mark. "Mr. Norris's lost letter!"

Mr. Claggett took it from him. "Yes, that's the one," he exclaimed. "How did it get in Rose's parasol? You know, Mr. Ficklin, I was ill that morning Mr. Norris left the letter here. But I'm sure I must have placed it on the table as I always do when I have anything for the rider."

"Yes," cried Rose excitedly. She seized the letter and put it on the table. "It must have been lying like that. When Mark and I came in and you weren't here, we were upset. We didn't notice the letter. But as I walked by I must have brushed it off the table, this way, and into my parasol."

"And it's been there ever since," finished Mark.

Mr. Ficklin picked the letter up. "Mr. Claggett," he said soberly, "I've been very unfair to you. The letter was not lost due to any carelessness on your part. And not only that, but I did not realize that the letter was lost when you were sick and alone here. I certainly shall see to it that the officers of the Express Company know you are not to blame for the loss of the letter."

Mr. Claggett's face lit up. "Mr. Ficklin, that means a lot to me. Now I have the money to pay

[ *179* ]

*"Congratulations on your sale of the mine!"*

Mr. Norris for his business loss. But I hated to leave the Pony Express with that black mark against my name. I can't tell you how happy I am that you were here when we learned the truth."

Mr. Ficklin and the Claggetts went outside.

"I probably won't see you again," Mr. Ficklin said, as he swung up into his saddle. "Thank you again for your loyalty and hard work. Congratulations on your sale of the mine, and good luck always to you!"

"Good luck to you!" the Claggetts answered. Mr. Ficklin rode off.

"And good-by to the Pony Express," Mark added.

"We have a few more weeks to go," his father reminded him.

"Yes, but it's really over," Mark said. "I'm sorry. But, oh, how glad I am that we were part of it from the beginning to the end."

And so in November, 1861, the Pony Express stopped running after about eighteen months of service. Its importance to a nation in distress will always be remembered. It helped to keep California in the Union. It showed that the Central route across the western plains was the best way for communications to go, and the telegraph wires followed this route to California.

The Pony Express never made money for its owners, but it brought lasting tribute to the riders and the station keepers and hostlers. The Pony Express is gone, but the galloping hoofs of its ponies will always be heard in the imagination of those who like brave men and flying mustangs.

## About the Author

WILLIAM O. STEELE was born in Franklin, Tennessee, and grew up with a great interest in our pioneer past. He graduated from college in 1940 and spent the next five years in World War II. In 1943 he married but was not discharged from the army until his oldest child was nearly a year old. As she grew older, he read to her, and this led to his becoming an author of children's books himself. He now has three children and has written several very successful stories of pioneer days, among them, THE STORY OF DANIEL BOONE, WE WERE THERE ON THE OREGON TRAIL, FRANCIS MARION, YOUNG SWAMP FOX; and WINTER DANGER. He and his family now live on Lookout Mountain, Tennessee.

## About the Illustrator

FRANK VAUGHN comes from New Rochelle, New York, where he went to school and later won two scholarships to the New York Phoenix School of Design. He has done extensive magazine and advertising illustrations as well as art work for numerous children's books. While in the navy he was stationed in the West, and since has specialized in Western subjects, which was why WE WERE THERE WITH THE PONY EXPRESS particularly appealed to him. Mr. Vaughn now lives with his wife and three children in New City, New York.

## About the Historical Consultant

SYLVESTER VIGILANTE was born in New York where, as a boy, he sold newspapers on the Bowery. He never finished school, but his love of books was so great that eventually he became the head of the American History Room of the New York Public Library. His knowledge of the West and its famous outlaws and sheriffs has proven invaluable to Western story writers all over the nation. When, after forty-seven years, he retired in 1953, he planned to do a lot of hunting and fishing; but fortunately the lure of books was too strong, and he is now Bibliographer of the American Historical Society.

# WE WERE THERE BOOKS